It's Simply Business Credit

For Aspiring Entrepreneurs, Government Contractors, and Franchise Owners

C. Naomi Covington

About the Author

Ms. Covington was raised in a diverse community of the southside of Monroe, LA where she found her inspiration and passion for entrepreneurship. The fearless African American pioneers in her small community motivated her immensely. These men and women were advocates for the advancement and empowerment of people of color. They were from all walks of life, from civic leaders, attorneys, electricians, physicians, pharmacists, to plumbers, and auto mechanics. Their stories and struggles had a profound impact on Ms. Covington as she started carving her path to success in life.

As a youth she was a Girl Scout who sold, Girl Scout cookies for Troup #102. It was exciting for to earn a commission on the cookies sold, something she looked forward to every year. This is where she began to hone in on her entrepreneurial tendencies. In 2007, she started her first business. Ms. Covington was in her early 20s then, but she had the foresight to set up a consulting and contracting firm that soon started doing business with the federal government. This was when she realized the importance of entering into government contracts and how lucrative they could be to anyone who knows what they are doing. Of course, Ms. Covington had her fair share of challenges along the line. It taught her the importance of perseverance and hard work. She also learned how to build stong relationships with creditors and effective ways to manage and leverage business credit.

Many entrepreneurs and small business owners struggle with managing their business credit. If you know how to handle that, you've already won half the battle. And that is why Ms. Covington has written this book. She intends to share with the world all she has learned about business credit through her trials and tests so that others can benefit from the knowledge.

Preface

"It's Simply Business Credit" is written for aspiring entrepreneurs, startup business owners, and those businesses alike seeking to build and grow. There is no guarantee to the success of your business. But success can begin with a strong business credit foundation. Building business credit and obtaining access to the capital needed to create a thriving business is essential to an organization's success. This book is going to help you in finding ways to build a heavy-duty credit line and managing your business effectively.

Contents

About the Author..*i*

Preface...*iii*

Chapter 1 ....*1*

ABCs of Business credit...

Chapter 2 ....*13*

Capitalization of business Credit...

Chapter 3 ....*26*

Mistakes You Need to Avoid ....

Chapter 4 ....*45*

Increasing the Value of Your Business ....

Chapter 5 ....*70*

Leveraging Business Credit for Growth ....

Chapter 6 ....*96*

Capital and Financing for Small and Mid-Sized Businesses...

Chapter 7 ....*121*

Maintaining an Immaculate Business Credit Score...............

Bibliography *160*

Page Left Blank Intentionally

Chapter 1
ABCs of Business credit

27% of business owners, as surveyed by the NSBA, claimed that they couldn't receive the funding they needed to grow their business. (Swype Fast) This statistic shows that business owners often find it challenging to finance their operations and future growth. Entrepreneurs face difficulties as a new start-up involves several challenging steps, from gathering funds and saving money to hiring workers and selling products.

However, did you know that in all these considerations, gathering business credit often takes the backseat? I believe that it is an essential part of any business as it can impact the overall growth of the company. Surprisingly, business owners of all ages fail to pay enough attention to maintaining business credit. 46% of all small businesses use personal credit for bearing professional expenses. According to research conducted by MasterCard, most small companies do not separate personal and professional expenses, which can

1

affect their growth and business development.

For instance, the most frequent impact that a lack of funding had was preventing entrepreneurs from growing their businesses. Therefore, entrepreneurs suffer from low credit score since they mix their personal and professional credit. According to a financial advisor for Small business owners, Meredith Wood; as a business owner, the mistake you don't want to make is thinking personal credit, and business credit is the same. There are many differences between them, as they inherently serve different purposes. Most of us know that good personal credit makes it relatively easy to get a mortgage and car loans.

However, in business, there is a whole other set of credit that can keep you worried. Understanding the difference between both can do wonders for you and your business. According to eBay store owner, Sophia Amoruso, *"much of my hard-earned success depends on my inability to accept failure as an option. I faced every challenge, be it about getting business credit or selling the idea."* Like, Amoruso, almost everyone aspires to run a small business that grows and turns out to as profitable. Entrepreneurship is one of the best jobs in the world, as it enables you to become your boss. As much as it seems attractive, there are multiple challenges attached to it. Out of all the problems, arranging business credit must take priority. In past years, financial institutions used to base credit decisions solely on personal FICO scores. Later in the book, we will talk more about FICO scores.

Nowadays, with increased globalization, business owners can build and improve the credit score for businesses that help in getting the most favorable financing opportunities. I would say if you are trying to start a business today, you can almost forget about going to a bank for financing.

Business credit and Personal Loans

Business credit and loans have emerged as an effective financing strategy for entrepreneurs. What does business credit represent? It is all about the ability, trustworthiness, and reliability of your company to handle money. Despite significant differences between personal and business credit, Meredith Wood also highlighted a few similarities.

Like personal credit, professional credit can facilitate you in quickly gaining finances. To briefly describe professional credit, I would instead say it is a value that represents whether an organization is an excellent candidate to lend money to, or do business with or not. Business credit scores, also called commercial credit scores, depending on a company's credit obligations and repayment histories with lenders and suppliers. It also reflects any legal filings such as tax liens, judgments, or bankruptcies.

The most appropriate way to know how long the company has operated, it's business type and size; and what is its repayment performance as compared to similar companies, is to evaluate its business credit. To further elaborate on the concept of commercial lending, this on it as the personal credit score of your business. This is a financial statistic which keeps a track record of your company's financial responsibilities. Many start-ups depend on the use of personal assets to secure initial business funding. As personal assets are often limited, the creditworthiness of the company decreases with the increasing load on the owner.

However, the use of business credit brings an essential economic resource which can strengthen the overall financial foundation of the company. Business credit can become a matter of concern for entrepreneurs because usually when you start a business, your friends are just starting too, which means you have access to a limited web of connections for obtaining monetary help in business. Budding entrepreneurs miss out on those well-placed connections that can easily recommend your firm to venture capitalists who in return can benefit you with business credit. This creates an organizational structure which stands on stable ground and allows the business to make an aggressive push.

While talking about business credit challenges for entrepreneurs, I must mention the case of Jon Henshaw, co-founder, and chief product officer of Raven Tools. According to Henshaw, the biggest challenge they faced at Raven Tools was the lack of business credit in 2013. This risk illuminated their strengths and faults like never before. He added that as we learned that the lack of business credit could affect our business, we immediately set out to fix our weaknesses and build upon our strengths. The challenge for them was 'fearing debt.' No one likes the feeling of owing money; however, to expand and grow business, it is vital to maintain a secure stream of money inflow. Are you wondering how business credit helped them in surviving? Well, it can play a significant role in upgrading large credit capacities. A business has around 10 to 100 times greater credit needs, as compared to personal credit. To make business creditworthy, you must position it as steady and robust because only then you will qualify for financing your projects and ventures.

Entrepreneurs can increase the value of their company with business credit. A creditworthy business has a commanding advantage in gaining financing abilities. With these financing instruments, companies can attract potential buyers. Here, I will further stress that developing business credit can offer remarkable benefits for a business and give a unique financial advantage within the marketplace. The availability of these assets can lead to secure lines of credit, financing, and leasing of much-needed equipment. If you too are planning to become an entrepreneur, you must carry out personal credit checks and secure your credit scores. The protection of personal credit can help you prevent personal debts and credit mixing with the company's assets. Before proceeding further, I must mention here that it's important to remember that if you sell the business with more significant business credit, it will have greater worth and will be easier to offload. Thus, it wouldn't be wrong to say that personal and business credit is essential for individuals planning to invest in an idea and starting a new venture.

Business credit is not limited to financing. Instead, as an entrepreneur, did you know you have a unique opportunity to develop, sustain, and acquire a loan, both individually and as a business owner? That's good news if you're planning to create, build, and grow a small business because then you won't have to rely solely on personal credit to do that.

The personal credit reporting agencies form a new credit profile when an individual with a social security number accepts their first job or applies for their first credit card. This profile is known as a credit report. This report is attached to every credit inquiry, credit application submitted, change of address, and change of job. The information is typically reported to the credit bureaus by those who are issuing credit. Eventually, the credit report becomes a statement of an individual's ability to pay back a debt.

The Need for Business credit

Before I talk about the importance of business credit for entrepreneurs, I must explain why businesses need credit. As an individual, we can never deny the significance of money in business. Credit allows companies to get money from financial institutions and use it to keep their operations running continuously.

Many small ventures trade-in cash because their customers pay in cash, and the owners settle the expenses using it. Business credit is ideal for entrepreneurs and individual professionals like fashion designers, consultants, real estate developers, investors, and builders since it allows them to buy raw materials and pay off their employees during their projects and business activities.

The same is true for businesses. When a business issues another business credit, it's referred to as trade credit. Trade or business credit is the single largest source of lending in the world. Many entrepreneurs are using this method for financing their ventures and business projects. The business credit bureaus, such as Experian gather information about trade credit transactions to create your business credit report using your business name, address, and federal tax identification number (FIN), also known as an employer identification number (EIN). You get this number from the IRS. The business credit bureaus, such as Experian, use this compiled data to generate a report that shows the financial worth and credibility of your company, based on previous business credit transactions.

Most times, those issuing credit to you will rely on your business credit report to determine if they want to grant you the loan as well as the amount of maximum available credit. The mistake many business owners make is using their personal information to apply for business credit, leases, and loans. By doing so, they risk having a lower personal credit score. At the same time, by using their credit history to get business credit, they're not able to build a strong business credit score which could have helped them attain critical business credit in the future. The key to establishing a business credit profile and a score is to find companies that will create a credit for your business without using your personal credit information and then report the payment experiences to the business credit bureaus like Experian. By publishing the information to the agencies, it'll help you establish your business credit profile.

The Big 3

In the business credit reporting space, there are 'The Big 3' who sell business credit reports. These are Dun & Bradstreet, Equifax Commercial, and Experian Business Credit. I have heard people say that building business credit doesn't matter. I mean, then why are many business credit reports pulled if it doesn't matter?

According to the Small Business Credit Survey from 12 Federal Reserve banks across the country, 61 percent of employer firms faced a financial challenge over the past year.

The main problem among them was the inability of a company to obtain business financing. The world is changing. I agree that ten years ago, business credit didn't matter too much. However, today, it matters. It's no secret that traditional bank loans are scarce even for the most successful small businesses, especially in the years since the financial crisis. For entrepreneurs and professionals, business credit can become a lifeline.

It enables you to successfully acquire funding for expansion, research, and development, capital expenditures, and staffing. Medical professionals, business developers, and consultants can use this credit for strengthening cash flow and earning better profits. With sound business credit, whether as an entrepreneur or a professional, you can gather the funds that are necessary for business survival.

According to Karen Gordon Mills, former administrator of the US Small Business Administration,

'*Banks are reluctant to process loans under $100,000, which accounts for most loans sought by small businesses. Therefore, where can small business owners go for the cash they need to grow and maintain their companies?*' In the first of this two-part series, we'll explore the pros, cons, and uses of the three standard financing options: business credit cards, term loans, and lines of credit. The first is the business credit card. Like a personal credit card, a small business credit card is a revolving line of credit you're expected to repay within the month.

We know that starting a business is challenging because the lack of business finances can keep you worried. However, understanding the difference between business and personal credit can help us in determining how to gather funds and start new ventures. I want to stress that all professionals and entrepreneurs must understand and focus on obtaining business credit.

Keeping your business finances separate from your risk is an ideal practice under all circumstances. As the discussion will proceed, we will look at the capitalization of business credit to understand how it is utilized and how the business credit should be set up.

Chapter 2
Capitalization of business Credit

In the previous section, we have thoroughly looked at the need for business credit for entrepreneurs using the examples of Big 3. We also looked at the types of business credit available for entrepreneurs, as well as how they differ from obtaining and using personal loans. We now know that business credit is different from the private credit system because it is one of the quickest and easiest ways to get money for running your newly formed business.

Business credit can help you in expansion, marketing, start-up activities, and other daily operations. Understand that establishing secure business credit can offer you one more option for generating monetary funds for a business. Almost every entrepreneur planning to start a business is concerned about gathering enough finances not only to begin but maintain positive cash flow. Every other entrepreneur has no clue how they can gather funds for their corporate venture. Therefore, I will talk about the types of business loans that they can use for financing their businesses in this chapter. The reason I am writing this book is to help readers comprehend how and where they can utilize these loans optimally. With all the knowledge and experience I have obtained in this field, I found what entrepreneurs don't understand is that business credit can be *cheaper* than personal credit.

With business credit, you are not only able to gather funds, but you can also form a clear distinction between business finances and your finances. Don't forget that mixing business and personal funds can produce disastrous results for you, especially if your venture fails. Now, knowing the list of way-outs you have when you are stuck in financial stress, can save you from burning personal credit.

I recently read a research work which explained the rate of start-up failures. The statistics show that about 90% of the new start-ups fail. This indicates that there must be something wrong, as most startups are not backed by large investors that can pour in millions of dollars in innovative business ideas although I do realize that you cannot achieve success in start-ups without stumbling with a few rocks or facing hurdles on the road to success. However, business owners can avoid the same mistakes that other entrepreneurs have already made by sticking to better financial practices and improved fund control. Upon investigating and looking at the odd reasons for this failure, I realized the critical reason behind decreasing success of start-ups is the lack of credit or financing.

Businesses often fail when entrepreneurs don't have enough funding for growth in critical areas like operations, marketing, and running finances. In my opinion, financing a business is often overwhelming for business owners because there are many options to fund a company with different rules. It is also the case of a lack of knowledge as most entrepreneurs do not have prior experience of dealing with business credit of any kind.

Types of Business credit

We need various types of business credit because

they are required to bring a corporate idea to life. For that reason, I would like to elaborate on the multiple types of business credit available for entrepreneurs. Being an entrepreneur, you must know how the following types of business credit work as finance providers:

Cash Flow Based Financing

Cash flow refers to the movement of cash or funds among different parties. In business, such financing refers to ensuring that there is always enough cash available in the accounts to remain positive during the operational phase. A small business owner can manage its finances ideally by ensuring that the balance of payments is supported by additional cash present in the business account. Now, banks and other financial institutions provide financing based on the cash flow records of a business. If your business is bringing steady income monthly, the bank will lend finances to pay for any immediate cash flow needs.

Asset-Based Financing

Many business owners and entrepreneurs can fail to

recognize that their current assets can bring them the required business financing. They can receive capital from the bank based on their venture's accounts receivable, machinery, equipment, and real estate value available as collateral. Simply speaking, the loan that you acquire is secured by the company's assets. These assets can provide a smooth flow of cash and ensure that business activities have a smooth run in. Most of your asset-based loans are structured to work as revolving lines of credit.

Equity Financing and Crowdfunding

If you are looking for different ways to finance your business, equity crowdfunding can become one of your best options. This is how: Equity crowdfunding forms a vital example of online offerings of the private company's securities to a particular group of people.

With this type of business credit, you can sell your company's securities in the form of equity shares, revenue share, debt and convertible note, and more equity crowdfunding options. Crowdfunding allows you to use small amounts of capital funds from a large number of individuals to finance a new business venture. One of the most common examples of this funding is the Shark Tank American Series. The show offers opportunities for budding entrepreneurs to get the desired financing to bring their dreams to fruition, in this reality show from executive producer Mark Burnett. This show provides a platform to people to present their ideas to the sharks who are five titans of the startup industry, who made their dreams a reality and turned them into lucrative empires. In return, investors or fund providers get business equity and profit shares. Now when you are scrolling through your funding options while stressing about your startup, I suggest you should not forget about the possibility of obtaining equity crowdfunding.

Business Credit – Unsecured Credit

Another option that I want to share is that of unsecured business credit, which does not depend on tangible collateral. For me, business credit can turn out to be an ideal way of financing business during its formative years. To get this funding, you want to ensure that your business hierarchy and working structure is finalized. You can also obtain personal business credit cards, especially if you have a poor credit history. Getting a credit card tied to your business allows you to successfully build business credit and get an improved cash flow situation in the future. I have also learned that every business owner is different as they are pursuing different goals and targets. However, regardless of their diverse intentions, they'd always prefer having some extra cash in hand for a variety of professional needs. Likewise, I also believe that businesses applying for unsecured business credit must pick the right ones because you'd only be able to see the significant advantages of that card when your finances are advancing.

Business credit cards are convenient and easy to qualify for, make online transactions easier, provide a financial cushion for emergencies, and can make accounting simpler for people with little knowledge of finances. They often come with rewards like cash back and benefits like flexible repayment terms and massive sign-up bonuses. You can also add multiple users to your account, allowing them to make purchases on your firm's behalf. On the contrary, I must mention it here that with interest rates topping 15%, credit card debt is costly. The CARD Act, which took effect in 2010 to reform the credit industry that removes practices like raising interest rates on existing accounts, does not apply to business credit card services. Also, you are personally liable for credit card debt even if taken in the name of a business. Therefore, it is essential to use cards responsibly.

Business Financing

Last but not least, to gather funding for your start-ups, you can opt for small business financing options. I suggest that you find suitable investors that are willing to partner with business professionals. Business financing is the way of obtaining money for starting a new venture. It refers to the investment that entrepreneurs can use by sharing ownership from the get-go. However, I have found that small business financing has decreased considerably in the last few decades.

Utilizing Business credit

We know and understand where our personal credit scores stand month-to-month, and how the personal credit impacts our ability to qualify for financial products successfully. Apparently, as a new business owner, we might not know anything about our startup's business credit ratings. These ratings can help us gather the desired funding for our business, which can benefit us in expanding and scaling the operations.

Before setting out to gather business credit, we must plan and arrange how we are going to utilize them. Many business owners will be surprised that knowing how to use business credit can help you plan tax credit and find out how you can make the ideal tax deductions.

Setting the Foundation of the Business

For every entrepreneur, it is essential to understand the process of establishing the foundation of the business. Research studies have revealed that over 95% of companies fail within their first five years in business, which should come as a shock to you if you are planning to start your business.

The statistics indicate the lack of capital as the primary reason for venture failure. The unavailability of liquidity stops the business growth and makes it increasingly difficult to sustain it in the initial phase. Before considering the credit options for a business, you must comprehend how to build a strong foundation for it. Building a strong foundation for our small businesses can help us separate business life from personal life. The process of setting up a business will require you to establish funding guidelines and apply for an EIN which stands for 'Employer Identification Number.' This registration is necessary because it adds you as a potential candidate for getting funds from numerous places. EIN is a unique nine-digit number assigned by the internal revenue service (IRS) to different business entities operating in the United States for identification. It often marks the first step in establishing a business in the country.

After successfully establishing the funding guidclines, new businesses must apply for tax-exempt status. The process will help you raise money for your firm by keeping it separate from your finances. I also assure you that it also opens up more avenues for obtaining the ideal business credit.

Credit Lines

Like many professionals, you must wonder how business credit like credit lines can help you generate business profitability, especially for a new venture. Let's look at it in this way, as you prepare for a sales push, a business line of credit is ideal for overcoming short-term working capital needs, such as inventory purchases. I am sure that you will require it once in a while, especially in the first two years of your business.

This is particularly effective and fruitful for seasonal businesses that need an inventory before they have the money to pay for it. Business credit is not just about getting access to financing. They have increasingly become the primary vehicle for setting terms on business loans, determining insurance premiums, and even setting lease payments. Good business credit can earn you lower rates, strengthening your cash flow as a result.

It's also true for businesses with inventories that turn over quickly, where a long-term loan is less desirable. It allows you to use wholesaler discounts and available limited offers by using the cash flow that you have available in the present.

With a line of credit, you can handle all such situations. You can make your inventory purchase now at a bargain price, then sell it once it's in season. Once that inventory is sold, and you've made a profit on it, you can repay your line of credit and use it again at a convenient time. Whatever your plans for using your line of credit may be, do not treat it as a long-term solution for your financial woes. Instead, think of it as a short-term source of cash, which is there when you need it, and when used responsibly, can help you maintain a sustainable path to growth.

A line of credit can offer ease of access to cash for equipment purchases; for example, if you need to purchase a new piece of foodservice equipment to meet the needs of your growing restaurant business. A line of credit is best used for smaller purchases. As interest rates aren't fixed, they can fluctuate with market conditions and your repayment history. This could lead to higher payment overtime on high-ticket or significant equipment purchases. In cases like these, a term loan may be a better option, since rates are fixed, though these are harder to get.

As you weigh up your options, calculate how much cash you'll need upfront. If you have time to pay off the purchase or it doesn't have a considerable price tag, a line of credit can be a useful option. For example, Fundbox Direct Draw allows you to draw funds in increments over $100, up to your credit limit, whenever you like – so you can pay off the cost of your equipment upfront or over a specific period.

When the sales momentum slows down, no amount of planning and preparation can prepare you for the challenges of a quiet season, such as meeting payroll. Laying off employees or reducing their work per week during this time isn't an option for growing businesses that need experienced employees always on staff to plan for and be available for busier times.

If cash flow is tight, and you don't have cash reserves, a line of credit is a useful safety net that can help you make payroll during slow times. With funds transferred as soon as the next business day, a line of credit gives you the flexibility to meet short-term payroll needs. Once your busy season starts, you can repay and continue onward and upward.

Chapter 3
Mistakes You Need to Avoid

Are you an entrepreneur running a business? Most of us have a dream to become self-employed, and one of the ways we can achieve this is by turning our savings into real investments such as establishing a successful business. Part of weaving this dream is to build the creditworthiness of the company itself.

If you're like most entrepreneurs, investors, and business owners I've met over the past 15 years, you're in danger. You're at risk of facing severe problems like getting hounded by creditors, denied a mortgage, declaring bankruptcy, losing your house, and paying more than your fair share of interest on your loan over several years. And it's all because of your business failures. Entrepreneurs typically make one or more financially devastating mistakes when financing the launch, operation, and/or growth of their businesses.

In most cases, they don't realize that they're making a mistake. And to tell you the truth, even when they know they're making a mistake, they calm themselves into thinking that the consequences will be a minor annoyance; until one day, they can't qualify for a mortgage. Or they can't get the to-die-for financing offered on the new car they're buying. Many failed business owners regularly face problems from creditors and eventually have to declare bankruptcy.

A good business credit score comes with so many advantages such as low-interest rates on business loans, lines of credit, business credit cards, and supplier financing. Also, a good score can get you higher credit limits, low insurance premiums, and attract more credit opportunities from lenders and existing suppliers.

However, not all business owners have a good business credit score. This is primarily because of small mistakes while working with their credit cards. These little mistakes are committed unknowingly, but when the report reaches the eyes of the business credit reporting agencies, they damage your business's credit score. Today, we will take you through 10 mistakes that can hurt your credit score. I will show you how to avoid them for a better credit score for your business. It's time to review those costly errors that can damage our personal credit scores and put our assets at risk. Now I know applying for a business credit card may not be the most exciting thing to do, but it's necessary and requires your careful attention.

To help you avoid these chilling and all-too-probable consequences, I've assembled a list of the nine most devastating financial mistakes entrepreneurs make. These are critical errors that can bury your business, smother you in personal debt, and destroy your financial future.

Our business-financing experts have helped thousands of entrepreneurs just like you avoid these expensive blunders while building substantial, valuable corporate credit—and along with it, the business of their dreams! Follow our time-tested ways of preventing these nine entrepreneurial dream-killers, and you'll be on your way to a more secure, satisfying, and financially rewarding future.

Personal Guarantee

You can avoid a personal guarantee with specific credit card issuers if your business has established secure business credit files. You can also prevent supplying a PG with individual secured business credit cards. By removing your assets and those of your supporters, you ensure that your business credit always remains separate from personal finances.

Opportunity Cost Recognition

At the first sign of profits or the first influx of credit, many business owners spend more than they have—or even more than they will make—on material goods. Lured by the luxury car or an exotic vacation they've lusted after for years, they ignore long-term business goals in favor of temporary and immediate gratification.

But if you want to achieve your long-term business goals, recognize that corporate credit and profits should be only leveraged to create more significant gains for your business. Instead of figuring out how much profit you can take out of the company, seek ways to invest your earnings back so that it will deliver higher returns for your business. This is not, by any means, a comprehensive list of all the mistakes entrepreneurs make in building corporate credit. However, if you address these costly and dangerous errors, you will be on your way to creating a safe, secure, and financially sound business: the business you always dreamed of!

Conducting a Credit Assessment

Before you apply for a business credit card, always find out first your current credit position both on a personal and a corporate level. Get copies of your personal credit reports and scores from the three major consumer credit agencies. Do the same with your business credit files and make sure that you have the ideal knowledge at your disposal.

Credit Building Process

Once they follow the prescribed process for building corporate credit, many entrepreneurs don't do enough follow-up work. If you don't keep track of your progress during the process of building excellent corporate credit, you may miss critical elements that could make the difference between getting the line of credit you desperately need. It is always a good idea to delegate, especially if you are busy. But be careful about what kind of work you entrust to another individual. In my experience, the work that directly affects the growth of your business and your wealth deserves your attention.

Personal Assets at Risk

Each time you pledge your assets for any credit extended to your business, you jeopardize your personal belongings, such as savings and investment accounts, car, and even your home. If your business can't pay off its debt, the bank will come looking for you to make good on loan. A business entity established as a sole proprietorship is the most susceptible to this risk.

Although you can build business credit as a sole proprietor, you will be liable for all personal and corporate debt instruments. Your credit history is based solely on activity associated with your social security number because you will not have a corporate tax ID number. As a sole proprietor, you also have no legal means for separating corporate and personal credit. The best way to protect your personal assets is to incorporate your business. You'll shield yourself from personal liability for the company's debts, and typically, this will also reduce your tax burden.

Business Corporate Credit

Corporate credit can be an invaluable tool as you build your wealth; because it gives you the flexibility to invest money in ways that you have determined will help you develop your business. But just as it takes time and patience to build wealth, it takes time and patience to make the corporate credit that enables you to get cash from lenders without your guarantee. Incorporating your business is just the start of the process. The industry standard for building corporate credit to the point where you can secure cash without a personal guarantee is two to three years.

We have streamlined its credit-building process so you can get the corporate credit you need in as little as one month (as long as you meet the criteria, if you don't qualify, don't worry, we will help you understand what changes need to be made to help you qualify). Then follow the steps to position your company to be eligible for no personal guarantee forms of credit.

Corporation and Building Corporate Credit

Many business owners are unaware of the value of incorporation. Even fewer understand the essential steps necessary for building the corporate credit that will enable them to take full advantage of their entrepreneurial status. Incorporation makes your business entity separate from you, the business owner— an independent entity with its own liability.

Incorporation separates your business assets from your personal assets. If someone sues your company, they cannot touch your house, car, or anything else owned by you or your family. But eliminating your personal liability for your company's debts and actions isn't the only reason to incorporate your business. Let's face it. You are in business to make money. And to make a profit and sustain your business, you need capital in the right place, at the right time to help your business grow.

By incorporating your business, you enable your business to establish corporate credit, which will ultimately provide the funds you need to grow your business, and one day, get to where your business can receive funding without personal guarantees. Keep in mind that this takes time to accomplish. But incorporating your business doesn't automatically qualify you for all the corporate credit you need, much less the best type of business credit. Your goal should be to secure cash lines of credit that are tied to particular stores or vendors for which you do not need to offer a personal guarantee.

To secure this *"Holy Grail"* of corporate credit, you need to follow a well-defined, step-by-step system to build your corporate credit history and business credit score. Some preliminary steps that every entrepreneur needs to take to secure excellent corporate credit include incorporating your business, maintaining a physical office, getting a local phone number and a business license, and have a business that produces real and measurable revenue. These steps pave the way for building your credit score with business credit bureaus. After you follow these preliminary steps and provide the bureaus with the information they require and go through our Corporate Credit Builder Program, you will be prepared to approach the handful of lenders who will give you a cash line of credit with no personal guarantee. In other words, those few lenders will help you keep your business and personal assets separate and provide you the cash flow you need to grow your business.

Family Money and Property Usage

When you use your personal credit card to buy business items, you instantly reduce the amount of credit you have available to get the things you and your family need and want. And if you, like many Americans, regard your credit cards as the financial cushion that will carry you through emergencies—such as an illness that makes it impossible to work—wasting your credit on business expenses weakens your safety net.

Still, many entrepreneurs ignore the dramatic consequences of this dangerous practice:

- They buy business-related items with their personal credit cards hoping to pay themselves back one day.
- They get other personal credit cards, leases, loans, and lines of credit, and then use them for business expenses.
- And, once they max out their borrowing limits, they persuade their spouses or other family members into using their credit to continue financing the business.

If you convince your family members to finance your business, you're just digging a deeper hole for your family to crawl out of. If your business fails like 95% of business do in the first five years, according to the Small Business Administration—your family could be wiped out financially. Don't ask family members to use their personal credit to invest in your business.

As we discussed above, using your personal credit to pay for business expenses is a strategic error. And if it makes little sense for you as a business owner, it makes even less sense for family members. Keep everyone's credit strictly separated from your company's corporate credit.

Unpaid Bills

You misplaced your credit card bill and sent in payment a few days late. It happens to the best of us, right? As an entrepreneur, you can't afford even a single late payment, whether in business or personal practice. Your credit file is a complete history of your credit activity. Not paying your bills on time can ruin your record altogether. Single delinquency can be held against you for years and then used to deny new credit which can make or break your ability to finance the launch, operation, and growth of your company.

There are two things you should do to protect yourself from this critical mistake. The first is to ensure that you pay your bills promptly. Second, keep your personal credit separate from your corporate credit. That way, problems with your personal credit history will have no bearing on your corporate credit. But if you do not take all the necessary steps to separate your corporate and personal loan, problems with your credit file could directly affect your ability to build your corporate credit and your business as a result.

Credit Contamination

When people marry, they vow to share their lives. For some good-hearted but financially naïve couples, this means sharing personal credit too. Unfortunately, adding your spouse to your credit isn't a show of undying loyalty and devotion. It's a recipe for credit file contamination which is an almost unforgivable sin if you're a business owner. When you initiate joint credit, your spouse's credit history becomes part of your credit file. If your spouse misses a payment, the delinquency affects your credit too.

The matter is complicated further if you haven't taken steps to separate your personal credit from your company's corporate credit. Credit file contamination created by a spouse's credit history could easily keep you away from achieving your business goals because it will prevent you from securing the financing necessary to grow your company. To avoid credit file contamination, keep your credit history completely separate from your spouse's history.

Even if your spouse ruins his or her credit, then you'll still have a good credit history to support your family as well as your business.

Personal Credit to Finance Your Business

The hands-down biggest and most common mistake entrepreneurs make, is using personal credit to finance their business ventures. Common examples include:

- Paying for business expenses with your personal credit cards.
- Obtaining personal loans to finance your business expenses.

If you've used one or more of these financing methods to fund your entrepreneurial ventures, I'm not surprised. Shockingly, many business start-up experts recommend these methods for financing new businesses. Their advice is well-intentioned, but incredibly dangerous. The reason for not using your personal credit for business purposes is simple: You WILL destroy your personal credit. It's inevitable. The percentages speak for themselves.

By using your valuable personal credit for business expenses, you run the risk of:

- Lowering your personal credit score. When you personally guarantee business-related financing, the lender will require a personal credit check. Every time an inquiry into your credit history is made, your personal credit score takes a hit. The lower your score drops, the harder it is to secure financing, especially financing with the most favorable terms.

- Reducing the amount of credit available for personal use. The more credit you have personally guaranteed for your business, the higher your debt-to-income ratio soars and the less that lenders will be willing to give you for personal use. Signing that loan for your business could prevent you from getting a mortgage on the new house you plan to buy a year from now.

- Losing everything. When you use your personal resources or credit to finance a business, you chain your financial security to your company's success. If the company fails, you'll be left holding the bag, and your personal finances will sink along with your business. You'll never recoup the *"loan"* you took from your retirement account to get your business launched. Creditors will be calling you for payment. And if things get bad enough, you may have to declare bankruptcy. To protect your financial security, I suggest that you don't use your personal credit to finance your business activities. Instead, take action to secure credit in your company's name – Without Risking Your Personal Assets, Lowering Your Personal Credit Score, and eventually, without a Personal Guarantee.

Use of the ideal business credit cards can be an excellent way for small business owners to grow their companies and to improve credit scores as well. However, if a business or company is not doing well, credit cards can create an abnormal financial burden for them. This way, the handy financial tool can become a liability for small businesses. As a small business owner, you can easily turn the benefits of credit cards for business into drawbacks, if you are not using the credit cards in the right way. Always keep in mind that not all credit cards are suitable for business use, as they are not created equal. Personal and business credit cards are two different things and also offer benefits accordingly. Choosing the wrong credit card for your business can be one of the biggest mistakes that you can make; it destroys your business's credit score and affects it for a long time adversely.

Now we know that if you are thinking that using a debit card as a reasonable choice to pay business-related costs to avoid business debt in terms of credit card bills, you are making a totally wrong decision that can harm your business credit scores. When using a business credit card to pay your bills and other business-related expenses, you enjoy complete protection in the case of billing disputes and fraudulent activities that a debit card cannot offer.

The use of a business credit card is always a better option for businesses, as they help build business credit to secure business loan easily in the future as well. I will also say if you don't have a proper business spending plan on hand, you are more likely to spend on unnecessary business costs with your new shiny and high limit business credit card that can increase business debt, instead of getting your venture finances on the right track. That's why the unavailability of a proper spending plan is considered as one of the small business credit card mistakes that should be avoided immediately, by building a productive business spending plan or budgeting.

Investing in your small business is a good thing for its positive growth, but if you're spending without a plan, you are setting yourself up for abnormal financial trouble in the near future. Likewise, not applying for small business credit cards with annual fees is one of the biggest mistakes your business should avoid when paying business costs via business credit cards. Business credit cards with annual fees are always beneficial for businesses, as they usually offer a variety of benefits like lower interest rates, higher credit limits, and so on. Almost all companies can apply for instant approval credit cards with the annual fee plan to keep business finances on track.

As a small business owner, your personal credit score should hold importance to you. Avoid using any cards that connect to your personal credit history to avoid mixing personal and professional credit.

If you carry a high balance on your personal credit card even if you pay that balance off in time, the chances are higher that it will still hurt your overall utilization rate on the business credit card too by lowering your attached credit scores. Always apply for business credit cards that do not have any connection to your personal credit score.

Chapter 4
Increasing the Value of Your Business

Before we look at the different ways to increase the value of our business, let's discuss how to start and grow it in the first place.

Setting up Your New Business

The first step in starting a business is to select what industry you want to be in, or the product or service you want to sell. Brainstorm and always come up with many ideas. Choose something you have a passion for as running a business will take A LOT of your time. The most successful and profitable businesses solve BIG problems.

Choose a business that solves a problem and relieves people or a business's pain point. The bigger the problem you solve, the more relief from the pain you provide, and the more successful you'll be. You may want to check with friends and family to see if they'd buy what you're selling before you do anything else. Even use your social media to survey and ask people questions about how useful a proposed product/service can be, or how much they'd pay for it. Don't go all-in unless you know you have something that will sell. Once you know what your business will be, next, it's time to set up your actual company. To do this, think of a name for your business that's catchy, possibly short, easy to spell, and that the domain is available for the particular selection. Use Go Daddy to search for the domain, and consider only going with a company name that has a domain available. Also, try and make sure your name doesn't reflect that you're in one of those high-risk industries.

Once you know the domain is available, next check to see if the company name is available in your state. You can do this by searching in Google for *"Secretary of State MY STATE."* You can then easily search for the company name. If the name is available, follow the steps in your SOS website to set up a new entity. You'll need to choose from profit or non-profit, select an entity type, consider an LLC or S-Corporation. Registration prices vary based on state, start and complete the process; it only takes 5-10 minutes.

Congratulations, you now have your own business!

Setting up Your Business EIN and Getting Your Bank Account

One of the first steps in starting a business is to get your EIN with the IRS. This is FREE to get at irs.gov.

Make sure you keep your Articles and EIN documents somewhere safe; you will often need them both.

Once you have your Articles of Incorporation and EIN, you can then set up your business bank account.

You must set up your business bank account quickly because many lenders and credit issuers see your bank account setup date as the date your company opened. It serves as its *start date.*

You will be asked for several items when setting up your new account, including your entity papers, such as your Articles of Incorporation, completion of their application, proof of your EIN, your ID, and the initial deposit of $25-200 depending on the bank and business account type.

You must set up your bank account the right way to ensure it is so easy for you to get credit and loans in the future. Your company name needs to match your entity paperwork. Your company address also needs to be the same. Make sure your EIN is also the same on your bank account as it is on your EIN paperwork. It will take about 30 minutes to set up your business bank account. Most banks will require that you go into the bank to get your new account set up correctly.

When you leave, they will give you a folder with documents that outline the terms on your bank account and info to set up online banking. You will also go with temporary checks for the account.

Steps to Initially Setup Your Business

One of the first steps to take to set up your business is to set up your website, especially for digital service businesses. You can do this cheaply using a company like www.templatemonster.com, then use www.upwork.com to hire a contractor to put up your website. You'll need the website template you buy from Monster, the content for each page, the domain, and the hosting, which you can get from Go Daddy. Also, get a professional email address. You'll need to get a phone number from a place like Ring Central, get a toll-free number, as well as a fax number.

List your phone number with 411. List Yourself can help *(only need this before you apply for credit and financing) in this regard.* Get a business address from a place like http://www.regus.com/.

Get any licensing you'll need from your county and your industry. Make sure that your business name, address, and other details are the same on all of your documents.

Get your logo using www.fiverr.com or www.99designs.com!

Next, write out a short description of your company and what you do, with a call-to-action, such as visiting your website. This will be needed as you set up your business listings.

Set up your business online congruently with free

listings:

- https://www.google.com/business
- https://www.bingplaces.com/
- https://smallbusiness.yahoo.com/local-listings

Set up your social media channels as well on:

- Facebook business page
- Twitter
- LinkedIn company page, and your profile
- YouTube
- Instagram

Advertising Your Business Part 1

Your priority in starting a business should be to start making sales, and this should happen within your network first. Start promoting your social media channels and website to your friends and family and ask them for their business, and who else they may know. You may even want to set up an affiliate program to pay them for referrals. Also, consider local marketing as well, like going to homes or businesses door-to-door.

You can look into networking events you can go to, such as Chamber of Commerce or BNI. There are probably many other smaller ones in your area available as well. Maybe even start your own if you have a lot of connections. Connections are the key when you start, so try to think about who you may know as a *"connector."* Ask your friends and family as well, and even a few connectors can help you make a lot of sales early. The BEST way to market and sell is by teaching what you know. You train and educate how people can benefit from the results of your product and service delivery. If you are selling tax services, start educating on how people can file their taxes, and what they should know.

Teach people ALL that you know using free channels like Facebook, YouTube, and Twitter. You can make great use of LIVE channels, such as YouTube LIVE, Periscope, and Facebook LIVE. When you teach and educate you to build a loyal tribe, many of those will use your free information and better their lives and be your best testimonials. Many others will pay you for your services because they want to work with you. When you sell this way, people want to do business with you versus you trying to *"sell"* them on why they should.

They see you as a credible expert and trust and rapport is built with you, making the sale much more manageable. Having this means you'll have long-term success, or face possible failure without it. To get content, host a webinar every other week. Put that webinar on YouTube and Vimeo, as well as other free hosting sites, and make your video into an automated webinar. You can create emails and social media posts out of it and turn it into blog posts, free reports, and guides.

Create articles and use www.Fiverr.com to distribute them. Make smaller videos out of your longer video and spread them out, and make a podcast out of your recording. Also, promote all of this in your email drip sequence we'll talk about later, as well as through your social media channels. Use free distribution channels to distribute your content like social media and online educational courses.

This will not net you immediate sales, but it will build your following, and within 6-12 months, you'll see exponential growth. To make this work, you MUST have a good sales funnel.

Advertising Your Business Part 2

A proper sales funnel offers quality information through a drip sequence every few days, and it is essential for building a customer database and maximizing the effectiveness of your marketing.

This is more information that gives you credibility and builds trust and rapport. Your email sequence should have written emails, videos, webinars, and more.

Once created, your primary marketing goal is to get leads into your sequence.

Your leads will then cultivate through time, and many of them will buy.

This is especially true if you also include emails with calls-to-action, such as giving access to free consultations or sales.

Provide content 80-95% of the time, then sprinkle in some CTAs. You can start by writing 8-16 emails and deliver them once per week, and you can even use those emails as scripts for marketing videos.

After you've mapped out your plan and have your funnel started, it's time to start running some tests. Is your product and service well-received by consumers, do they like it?

Does it work, does it help solve a problem, and what feedback are you getting?

What's the best way to advertise and get a response, what's the best headline and message that gets people to respond?

What's the best media to advertise and get the best results? Chances are you won't know this early on, and you'll need live testing to get accurate answers.

Give out information, and use sources like YouTube, other social media, and webinar attendees to get a gauge on message and topics your prospects want to know more about. Use media that you can test small and cheap, like Facebook and Pay-per-click advertising to see what works. You must find out what message works, what ad body, and what images are the best? You can find out all of this just by testing small.

This is why you test and test small and cheap.

Does Facebook get you a better response than PPC, or is direct mail better?

What words in your headlines make all of the difference?

Test and find out!

Increasing the value of a business is essential for maximizing profit and sales.

After many years of working closely with mid-market businesses providing valuation, divestiture, and acquisition services, I have seen that many otherwise well-run companies are incredibly disappointed when it's time to sell because they either don't receive the valuation they expect or, even worse, they don't get any offers at all. With an aging baby boomer population, more businesses than ever will be looking for an exit. Buyers will have their pick of the litter. That's why sellers must make their businesses as attractive as possible. The strategies presented here will not only help you maximize value, but they will also be necessary to ensure that your business is scalable in the future.

Simple Keys to Maximize Value

It can be hard to focus on increasing the value of your business if you have no immediate intention of selling. There are so many other competing demands for your time. But for those proactive business owners who see the end game of cashing out at some point, three simple concepts will help you maximize the value of your business:

- Focus the most of your efforts on increasing cash flows

- Put yourself in the buyer's shoes

- Pick the best exit strategy when the time is right and execute immediately

Focus on Increasing Cash Flow

Cash flows are the number one factor that potential buyers look at to determine the valuation placed on an acquisition target. Buyers calculate the value of a business by estimating future cash flow and assessing the risk associated with generating that cash flow. A company that has a track record of sustainable or growing cash not only validates its product or service, but it also demonstrates the management team's ability to drive growth. Buyers pay more for the higher likelihood of future growth. Historical financial results are essential because they provide a good indication of what is possible.

Because of the importance of determining value, I can't stress enough the need for owners to prepare future cash flow projections for their business. Let's look at this logically. Would you rather have a potential buyer determine the value of your company from cash flow projections that *they* prepare or from ones that are made by you, with full support around why your projections are achievable? I think the choice is obvious.

Analyze Your Buyers

Even owners who are not planning on selling their businesses can learn a lot from how potential buyers perceive an acquisition target. Based on my experience, these are five areas buyers scrutinize the most when purchasing companies:

Strategic Planning

Quality businesses have a well-thought-out and documented strategic plan. A written plan gives any outside party (be it a bank, investor, or potential buyer) the confidence that a business owner knows where a business is going, and how it is getting there. If your business doesn't have a strategic plan, make one.

Strong Management

A properly trained and widely knowledgeable management team is desirable for any company. A truly valuable team is deep (you have several key players with job-specific experience), and the knowledge of the business does not reside with any one individual.

It is essential to assess the strength of your management team, honestly. Are you able to leave the business for extended periods and feel comfortable that the company will run as efficiently or even better than if you were there? If not, start building a better management team through training, improved corporate alignment, and, if needed, hiring. It may impact profitability in the short-term, but it will more than makeup for it by creating future value. On top of that, wouldn't it be nice to take an extended vacation with that peace of mind?

Diversified and Recurring Revenue Base

A company that has one customer representing 30 percent or more of its revenue is too risky for most potential buyers. If that customer were to leave, it would significantly impact revenue and cash flow. As such, customer concentration is an area that can have a significant impact on value.

Review your sales per customer. If the revenue is too

concentrated among a few customers, find a way to get more income from others. One of the best ways to do this is by establishing a recurring revenue service that also builds up your business value.

High Barriers to Entry

Barriers to entry can be created through intellectual property, such as patents or trademarks, economies of scale, significant capital investment, customer loyalty, supplier or distribution agreements. Companies that can deter competition from entering the market can better sustain a leading status. Find that unique element in your company and use it to create an economic moat to protect you from your fiercest competitors.

Scalability

Buyers like companies that make significant investments in systems to serve customers, produce products, and handle customer complaints efficiently. Scalable, measurable, and repeatable processes make it easier and less expensive to hire and train employees and allow you to serve your customers better. All businesses have functioning systems in place, but getting your employees to document and refine these systems will give your company the ability to grow much more quickly.

Pick the Right Exit Strategy and Execute

Selecting the appropriate exit strategy — and executing it — is a significant consideration for a business owner who wants to maximize value. The following needs to be considered:

Planning

To be successful at value creation, business owners must plan. When more time is available to implement these strategies, more value can be created. Working on these tools today will also allow business owners to evaluate and take advantage of the opportunities that present themselves in the future, like a favorable market environment (i.e., high valuation multiples) or unsolicited offers to be purchased.

Execution

Creating an effective auction process with the use of a professional intermediary is critical to achieving the appropriate deal terms and value. These experts will better position your company, support your valuation, get more qualified buyers to the table, and negotiate favorable terms. Other professionals, such as tax and M&A advisers, must be involved early in the process to maximize the after-tax income realized on exit. This is the time when a business owner's years of efforts are monetized; therefore, this process should not be taken lightly.

Timing

Even with proper planning and execution, if the market is not right for M&A activity, you might not find the best buyer or get the valuation you deserve. Be vigilant about staying on top of what is happening in the marketplace by talking to your bankers, accountants, and others who have their ears in the street. If you're ready to sell when the M&A market heats up, that's the best time to pull the trigger for value maximization.

Increase Your Chance of Success

These concepts sound simple, and I know most entrepreneurs intuitively realize them. The difficulty is staying focused and making these three simple ideas a priority in the day-to-day management of your business. Find any means necessary to help you remain dedicated to the worthy cause of increasing the value of your business. The rewards of being able to cash out on your terms (whatever they might be) are worth the effort.

Credit Policy and Business Value

A credit policy is a blueprint used by a business throughout the process of making a decision. This decision will help extend credit to a customer. Ultimately, the primary goal of a credit policy is to avoid extending credit to customers who cannot pay their accounts successfully.

A good credit policy must help people attract as well as retain customers without hurting the cash flows. Having a firm grip on the overall financial condition of your company is an essential responsibility of the owner. Determining the value of a business for sale is complex. There are many ways a company can be valued. Some valuation methods tend to work better for different types of businesses. It is essential to informally determine the value of firms that are considering sale or credit.

Credit terms set the time limits for customer's payments on the merchandise or services received. It is essential to learn how to create a clear policy, delineating when to extend credit to a customer. It will also determine how much credit we can continue with and for how long. Credit terms are simply the time limits you set for your computer's promise to pay for their merchandise or services received. Numerous small business owners can establish credit terms for improving businesses.

Customers tend to purchase merchandise or services that we expect to pay within a specific period. To increase the value of the business, focus on building a credit policy that works well with consistency. Longer credit terms mean businesses will have to wait longer for the cash inflows from the collection of accounts receivable. Similarly, it facilitates in offering trade discounts that can help speed up cash inflows from accounts receivable. It can help in reducing a cash flow shortage being created by extended credit terms.

A good credit policy should help you attract as well as retain customers without having any negative impact on your cash flow. From the cash flow perspective, a lower average investment can relate accounts receivable, which ensures a quicker inflow of cash for the company. It can help in offering increasing overall company cash flow. For the growing value of the business, it is essential to analyze economic conditions, location, and market and technological factors. Considerably, the economy affects all businesses in numerous ways. The economic factors can help in evaluating how the current environment affects your business. In different ways, a certain level of local economies can have a more significant effect on business.

For instance, it is challenging to place a value on the level of technology used by a company. It's a massive factor in the sale of a business. It is difficult to place a value on the level of technology a company uses. Still, it's a massive factor in the sale of a business. With website and businesses, online selling can strengthen the use of computer apps and programs. The best way to increase the business line of credit is to show that you need a substantial increase. It helps to clearly reflect why you need the funds and how they will be paid.

Here, I would say if you plan to sell your business, you must establish good business credit. For instance, if you are serious about looking for a buyer, remain mindful of the impact that selling the business will have on credit. The key to value business is managing credit. Business credit doesn't have to be a formal loan. I would say you can also acquire and build credit by working with suppliers. You can conveniently get goods and services on credit today. You don't have to pay until later. The model applies to numerous services, including office supplies as well as warehouse space. Another way of valuing a business is by providing information and monitor progress. It will help in building business' credit, which isn't exactly effortless.

You may have to provide information to credit bureaus, and you'll undoubtedly want to make sure they have accurate information and data about your firm. This will allow us to form discussions and agreements effectively. You've probably seen advertisements for 0% credit lines for $50,000-$250,000, or more. The 0% program is perfect for startup companies, high-risk industries, and those who don't have or want to provide proof of cash flow or collateral. So unlike asset-based lending, you don't need to show or provide assets as collateral for approval. Also, unlike cash advances, you don't need to be in the business for 6-12 months or have a consistent cash flow for approval. Another benefit is that you *only pay on what you owe…* not like a loan.

So if you get approved for $100,000, you won't make payments on $100,000, you only make payments on the balance you owe. So if you charged $4,000 on the account, you'd need to make payments on only that $4,000. And during the 0% interest period, you won't pay interest.

A significant benefit of this program is it's possible to get credit cards that *only report to the business credit reporting agencies*, not the consumer agencies. So you can use this credit, even with high utilization, and have no adverse impact on your consumer credit. This is a *BIG* deal because utilization is 30% of the consumer FICO score. If you use more than 30% of your limit on an account that reports to the consumer CRAs, you'll lower your consumer credit scores.

Another benefit is that the rates on this program are *0%,* for a limited time. That's a VERY important detail for applicants, as 0% and only paying on what you owe allow for lower periodic payments. This can be a big deal, especially for startups short on cash.

But *BEWARE!* Some sources don't mention that the 0% rates are only for a limited time. No loan, credit card, or credit line you'll find is 0% beyond an entry period; the interesting point is to discover how they make money. *EVERY* one of these programs you see only offers 0% for a limited time, usually 6-18 months, just like with consumer credit cards.

You can call the card issuer and try and extend the 0% intro period. Some sources who offer this program might even help you with this. Also, you can get more cards after that period expires, then balance transfer on to newly obtained 0% cards after that period as well. Just keep in mind the *ethical issues* in doing so to the card issuer. And also, be careful when working with sources who don't tell you upfront that the 0% is only for a limited time. Many promote this as if 0% is throughout the life of the program when it's not.

It's important to note that these are *not true credit lines*. They are credit cards. Many try to promote them as credit lines because this is what most entrepreneurs want. But these are simply credit cards where you can get multiple of which add up to $50,000, $100,000, and more. In the next chapter, as the discussion will progress, you will learn about leveraging business credit.

Chapter 5
Leveraging Business
Credit for Growth

Leverage is a business term that refers to how a business acquires new assets for startup or expansion. I would say leverage is a way to permit a company to expand. It can be a verb as in *"businesses leverage themselves by acquiring loans"* for expansion. When a business is leveraged, it means that the firm has borrowed money to finance the purchase of assets. In general, companies can employ leverage through equity by raising funds in cash from investors.

One way to leverage credit to generate wealth is by having a good credit score. Having good credit can save you thousands of dollars over the life of a corporate loan. Even just one percentage point can save you $20 to $300 a month. The money saved can be used to invest or borrow money to purchase assets to generate wealth. A good credit score, usually 700 or above, can help you in several ways, including the following:

- Increase your financing options
- Get the lowest interest rates
- Allow you to pay less for purchases
- Spur competition between companies for your business
- Invest in profitable opportunities
- Establish a solid credit rating
- Get approval for more substantial loans and higher credit limits
- Provide quicker approval times
- Look favorable when applying for a job

Here are five ways that you can leverage your credit to generate wealth:

You Should Become a Homeowner

Becoming a homeowner increases your credit score, proves that you are a responsible spender, brings a tax write-off, and provides you with an asset that will appreciate over time, which increases your net worth.

You Should Purchase Investment Property

Investment property provides cash flow that can be used to generate wealth and allows more opportunities to become available to you. Do the research and buy books on buying investment properties, join a real estate group, and listen to financial investment shows to find out the best way to get started.

You Should Start a Business

Discover what you love to do more than anything else. Do your research before starting your business and take small steps. Start your business in your home to get the feel of running a corporate venture. There are also many tax write-offs for home-based businesses.

You Should Use Venture Capital

Use venture capitalists to invest in your business. Venture capital is a fundraising technique for companies, who are willing to exchange equity in the company in return for money to grow or expand the business. VC firms often want a high rate of return 20%

or more and will finance the business, starting from $500,000 to millions of dollars. A venture capitalist also wants greater control of a company and a quicker return on their investment.

You Should Use An Angel Investor

Use angel investors to invest in your business. An angel investor is an affluent person who provides capital for a business start-up, usually in exchange for convertible debt (a bond that can be converted into shares of stock in your company) or ownership equity (remaining interest in all assets after all liabilities have been paid). If assessments of assets do not exceed liabilities, this will result in negative equity and cannot provide ownership equity.

The key to leveraging credit to generate wealth is to develop good spending habits, live within your means, and maintain a good credit score. The higher your credit score, the less you pay for a loan, and the easier it will be to establish business relationships, gain new clients, and generate wealth.

Case of Leveraging Business Credit for Growth

Using leverage to support business startup and growth is becoming increasingly common. Leverage is a business term that refers to how a business acquires new assets for startup or expansion. I must say leveraged credit or loan is a type of a loan that is extended to companies or individuals that have considerable amounts of debt of poor credit history. It is suitable for business because as the proportion of debt to asset increases, the number of financial leverage also increases. This can reduce the earnings per share of existing shareholders. The financial leverages have two primary advantages which can strengthen profits.

Like personal credit, there is always a right way and a wrong way to use a line of credit for your business. If in any case, it is done wrong, as using that line can add incremental stress to your cash flow and operations until you run out of space. As a result, you close down. On the other hand, if it is done right, it can give you what you need to create an upward spiral of cash flow. It can result in success and venture expansion.

It is crucial to learn the dos and don'ts of leveraging a business line of credit. I would say, 'Begin with the end in mind.' Lines of credit operate more like credit cards than loans because it can turn tempting to use your line of credit as a portable cash fund. On the other hand, it allows you to draw funds only when you have a specific organized and well-researched plan to make more money than you expect to spend in interest and fees.

Remember, don't fail to shop around for lines of credit. All business lines of credit aren't created equal. With all resources, getting more for less is the best definition we use for leverage. To properly leverage your business line of credit, it is vital to carry out a bit of comparison shopping.

Another example here is about making strategic plans. Remember we have access to funds made available by a business line of credit. These funds can contribute toward expansion, payroll, stocking inventory, and host of other corporate functions. For leveraging a business line of credit, it is essential for companies to transit to cash flow for funding when you are ready. Remember, more than one business owner has fallen into a pattern of relying on credit funds over and over. However, once your company has achieved a sturdy structure that leads to high performance, you must make a move to relying on your cash flow for expenses.

Example of DUNS

When you actually start applying for credit, you should consider using some type of business address or a virtual address, but setting up your entity and your D-U-N-S will require a physical address of some kind, as you can't use a virtual address. Also, even though you can obtain real business credit without supplying your SSN, most business bank accounts may require one to be opened.

You can search for your DUNS through the link at www.dandb.com/free-duns-number. During the DUNS setup process, you'll be asked for a lot of information. If you select that you're a government contractor, you'll get your DUNS in about 1-2 weeks. If you don't pay D&B anything and aren't a contractor, it can take up to

30 days to get your DUNS. The process to obtain your DUNS will require about 10-15 minutes. Once you're done, D&B will email you. Reps will also start to call and email you to upsell you to their D&B Credit Builder program. With Dun & Bradstreet, there are three ways to start building your business credit. The first way is by using their Credit Builder program at https://www.dandb.com/credit-builder/. This runs $159 monthly *(April 2017),* or they'll also often offer you a one-time fee that you can pay. They will offer to set up your D-U-N-S for you if you purchase, without you needing to wait 30 days to get it by mail.

With Credit Builder, you also get access to your D&B scores and ratings. It can add positive payment experiences to your report, give alerts when others inquire into your business, and see how your company compares to others in your industry.

With Credit Builder D&B allows you to add trade accounts you already have that aren't currently reporting to your D&B reports. These accounts then show as trade lines, helping you build your profile and score. This might be something to consider if you have a lot of accounts you pay now that can qualify and aren't currently reporting.

Keep in mind; this service is only to add accounts to your D&B reports, not Equifax or Experian, which many credit issuers and lenders use. Also, D&B isn't helping you access new credit. It is only helping you add existing credit to your reports. Also, keep in mind, many types of accounts cannot be added to your D&B using this Credit Builder Service, https://www.dandb.com/glossary/trade-references/.

From https://www.dandb.com/glossary/trade-references/, *"D&B works together with thousands of nationwide vendors that report payment experiences regularly. These data providers have requested to remain anonymous and cannot be added by a customer for a trade reference.*

Some types of companies do not respond to D&B's requests for information within a reasonable time frame. D&B will make six attempts to contact a company that has been selected to provide trade reference and will accept inbound referrals at any time. However, a customer may resubmit references at any time, after which D&B will make six more attempts. Some companies have proven over time to be less trustworthy. Accordingly, D&B has identified specific characteristics associated with companies and maintains policies related to the eligibility of that company to provide a reference." From https://www.dandb.com/glossary/trade-references/,

"The following kinds of trade references are amongst those that are not accepted by D&B. It includes payments that have not yet been made but are anticipated, payments to businesses that have shared principals or some other type of legal ownership relationship, financial services like banks, credit unions, and insurance, bank references, utilities and gas companies, credit card companies, landlords, virtual offices credit counseling or registered agents, international companies, and businesses with an unknown SIC."

So, before you buy, think about the accounts you may have who might report, such as your CRM or other types of software or other accounts that aren't restricted. Also keep in mind, getting D&B on the phone with your service provider isn't always easy. It can take time. If you do have good personal credit now or a personal guarantor, you can shortcut your business credit building process with all three reporting agencies. With UBF, you work with a funding source that specializes in securing business credit cards. This is a VERY rare, little known program that few lending sources offer. They can usually get you 3-5 times the approvals that you can get on your own. Individual approvals typically range from $2,000-50,000. Approvals can go up to $150,000 per entity, such as a corporation.

With UBF, they get you 3-5 business credit cards that report only to business credit reporting agencies. This is HUGE; something most banks and card issuers doesn't offer or advertise. The lender can also get you low intro rates, typically **0%** for 6-18 months, and they'll also get you the best cards for points, meaning you get the best rewards. You must have excellent personal credit now, preferably 685 + scores, the same as with all business credit cards. You shouldn't have ANY derogatory credit reported to get approved. You must also have open revolving credit on your consumer reports now. You'll need to have five inquiries or less in the last six months reported, and you can also use a guarantor.

All lenders in this space charge a 9-15% success-based fee. You only pay the fee off of what you secure. Remember, you get a ton of extra benefits and about 3-5 times more money with this program than you'd get on your own, which is why there's a fee, the same as in all other lending programs. You can get approved using a guarantor. You can even use multiple guarantors to get even more money. You can also build business credit using NEW accounts, instead of adding existing accounts to your D&B profile.

There are many benefits of building business credit as this way you don't need to buy Credit Builder, you don't need good credit, cash flow, or collateral, and you're building your business credit AND getting real, useable credit at the same time. At the same, you're building credit with all three reporting agencies.

Vendors are companies who will offer you credit, even if you have none now, and report to the business reporting agencies. They will provide you with Net 30 terms usually, meaning you have 30 days to pay off what you borrow in full. Some will offer Net 10, 15, 20, 30, or 45 days, and you can get approved even as a startup. Before you apply for vendor accounts, you should set up your business credibility first. Credit issuers and lenders have a *"secret"* set of requirements you must meet to get approved. These requirements are to determine if your business is legit and *"credible"*. You must ensure you meet these requirements before applying for any credit.

You must have a website and a professional email address. It should not be a Gmail or AOL type email. You must have a business phone number and not a mobile or home phone. You should have a toll-free number and fax. Your phone needs to be listed with 411, and you should be listed online, and all of your listings must be the same.

You need a real business address or virtual address or a home address, not a P.O. Box, or UPS address. Make sure you obtain all necessary licensing needed for your industry and state. You should be listed online, and all of your listings should be the same. Some vendors to start with who report to D&B and will approve you with no existing credit include Seton, Quill, Gemplers, and Uline. For REAL business credit, link it to your EIN, not your SSN. You shouldn't put your SSN on the application. D&B will want you to have 2-3 of these types of accounts to activate your profile and score. You do NOT need to pay D&B to have your profile enabled. You need to find items you want to buy, apply for credit, use that credit, and pay the bill on time. You should have five payment experiences to start applying for store credit. Most major retail stores offer EIN-only business credit, including Staples and Office Depot, Lowes and Home Depot, BP and Chevron, Best Buy, Apple, Dell, Walmart, Costco, and Sam's Club and most others.

With ten total payment experiences, you can start to secure fleet and cash credit cards based on your EIN only. Also, you'll have a much better chance of getting loans and credit lines. In some cases, you can even obtain lending such as auto leasing without a personal guarantee.

Building your business credit is a never-ending process. The more credit you apply for, the more you get it. Likewise, the more you use that credit, the higher your limits become. Keep in mind; ALL lenders review business credit when applying for business loans, even high-risk lenders.

The main credit score used in the business world is known as a Paydex score, provided by Dun and Bradstreet. From D&B, *"The D&B PAYDEX Score is D&B's unique dollar-weighted numerical indicator of how a firm paid its bills over the past year, based on trade experiences reported to D&B by various vendors."*

The Paydex score ranges from 0-100, with 100 being the best score a business can obtain. A score of **80** or higher is considered *"good"* or healthy credit. A business can get a good business Paydex credit score by ensuring payments are made promptly to suppliers and vendors.

Business credit scores are based only on whether the business pays its bills on time:

Expected payment may come early 100

Payment comes within the early discount period 90

Payment is prompt 80

Payment comes 14 days beyond terms	70
Payment comes 21 days beyond terms	60
Payment comes 30 days beyond terms	50
Payment comes 60 days beyond terms	40
Payment comes 90 days beyond terms	30
Payment comes 120 days beyond terms	20
Unavailable	UN

A true credit line is a line-of-credit that you get a debit card for and functions much the same as a credit card. Most credit lines don't offer 0% as these cards do, but credit lines do allow you to take cash out of the line at the same rate as the line is for, such as 8%. With credit cards, you can't take cash out on them, without paying a hefty cash advance fee of usually 20% or more. These are the primary differences between credit cards and lines. With this program, a lending source goes to work on your behalf and secures credit cards for you.

The company is not a lender or card issuer. Instead, they function as experts in obtaining credit cards, and go to work to apply and get you the most credit they can secure. In almost all cases, their tactics to get you credit result is much more than you can get on your own. There are a few reasons they can get you more credit than you can get on your own. For one, a bank or individual credit issuer will usually issue you credit for close to what your highest revolving limit is now. Moreover, they'll only grant you one card, not multiple cards. If you went to another bank and applied, and continued doing this, you'll get declined. The reason for this is because these banks and card issuers don't want to issue a credit to someone who's mass-applying for new credit in a short period. So even 2-3 inquiries on your consumer report within six months can disqualify you for this program, or for credit with any card issuer.

Many entrepreneurs think they can just go into their bank and get what this program delivers just because they have good credit. However, banks care about your consumer credit, business credit, and bank credit. Also, they want financial information for an actual credit line or loan. Moreover, those financials would have to show good revenues and profits for approval. So best case, without this, they'd only get you one credit card, no loan, and no credit line. With this program, the company you hire goes to work to get you up to five, usually, of the best and highest-limit cards you can get. They apply for them all at once, so they can get you five cards where if you used on your own you'd only get 1-2 max.

This means they can *usually get you five times the amount of your current highest limit account.* Comparatively, your bank can only get you one of these types of account, and they often don't report to the business CRAs.

There are two types of cards they can get you. One type is personal cards. These instruments report to the consumer CRAs. They can also get business cards. These don't report to the consumer CRAs.

Whether you get one or the other, how much money you can get is all dependent on one thing, and one thing only—*your personal credit quality.*

This type of credit is **unsecured**. Unsecured Credit is obtained with no security, or assets, or collateral. It is money that is lent where the lender has no guarantee to collect in case of default. Because there's no collateral being supplied, and they don't look or care about your cash flow either, all that matters is your personal credit.

To be approved, you need excellent credit as it is credit and credit alone that is being used for approval. Remember, *credit is ALL that is looked at for approval,* so they need outstanding credit to qualify, not just good credit.

If you have 650 type credit, you'll only get approved for PERSONAL cards. If you have 700+ scores, then you can get business cards.

Qualification Requirements are:

- Credit Quality
- No bankruptcies at all on the report
- Might get approved with BK, if it is not on the report

- No judgments; must be paid off
- No tax liens; must be paid off
- No credit counseling
- No late payments in the last 12 months
- No active outstanding collections in unpaid status, less than $500 MIGHT be okay
- At least one bank card with 3yr history or $3k limit, if no car loan or mortgage, they need two bank cards
- Balance/ Limit ratios on existing revolving accounts
- The lower the ratio, the higher the approval amount
- 30% ratio is required

Look at the overall percentage and specific percentage on each account credit inquiries to learn how much credit you can obtain. This is a significant factor that ties into approval. More than three inquiries within six months are too much. Lenders do not want to see the person is applying for new credit, especially not with other revolving accounts.

Limits on existing accounts determine how much $$$ you'll be approved for. The limit is directly proportional to new approval limits, maybe slightly higher. A person needs higher limit cards for approval, typically over $5,000 is reasonable. For example, a person with $500 limit won't be approved for $5,000, maybe only $600.

For instance, a person with $10,000 limits might see approvals of $12,000. Approvals can be $50,000 or higher. More partners mean more dollars. You can usually get five times that of your highest limit account. Most sources charge *9-12%* SUCCESS-based fees. This means you'll pay an average of 10% on the amount you borrow; 10k on 100k in financing. Keep in mind, *ALL lenders on ALL loan programs charge fees*. You'll easily pay 5% or higher even on an SBA loan. But this program, like most others including SBA, *"roll-in"* your fee, so you don't pay upfront.

Once you get your cards in the mail, then you are invoiced the fee. Usually, you'll pay the fee for each card you get as that card comes in, meaning you'll get multiple invoices. Also, most people use the cards they get to pay the applied fees.

Some sources do charge upfront. This can be dangerous because they have no real motivation to get you the most amount of money. Some companies will also let you pay upfront to enter the program, even if you don't have good credit. They sell you on the vision of helping you fix your credit so you will qualify in the future. Reliable credit repair takes time, usually many months to accomplish even then to get over a 700 from a 500 starting point is extremely tough to do. You must obtain good credit accounts to get good scores, which are needed for this program. So a real credit re-building process is not fast or secure, and there are other programs you can get funding with quickly that allow for credit issues without trying to *"fit"* into this program.

Also, keep in mind; it's not legal to charge upfront when credit repair is being provided according to the Credit Repair Organizations Act. You have rights when paying for credit repair, including not paying upfront. Only pay after *"service is fully performed,"* being supplied a proper contract with specific statements, and being provided three cancellation notices. Accurate info can't be disputed, and untrue statements are prohibited.

Some sources might charge you for inquiry removal. Be careful, in many cases; they are challenging accurate inquiries but claiming they are a fraud. This is illegal, and you can be on the hook for their actions. Some sources get high approvals right away. They work with and know underwriters who will approve your application, and they apply only at sources who will approve you. They even know these sources down to a regional level. Others get declines first, and then have to *"negotiate"* to even get you an initial approval. They do this by calling and pretending they are you. Even if successful, this process takes longer and usually nets you lower and lesser approvals. You can use a *"credit partner"* for approval.

This may be a partner, friend, or family member, who wants to use their credit to help your business get money. As an example, someone might want to get a piece of your company, in exchange for allowing their credit and guarantee to be used to obtain this type of funding. This is acceptable, and if you use a partner as well as your credit, you can get even more money.

These accounts DO require a personal guarantee from you. These are *not real business credit accounts* because they need a PG and proper credit for approval. Even though business cards report to the business CRAs and will help you build real business credit; but remember, YOU or your Partner is personally liable in case of default. You'll start your approval process by finding the best source. We have used almost all significant sources in this space and now only work with the absolute best references. By *"best,"* I mean the sources who will get you the most money at the fastest. These are sources who don't have shady practices. Once you find the best source, fill out their application, and to get access to our sources, you can do that here. You'll usually be contacted the same day or within 24 hours. When contacted, say what you are trying to accomplish, and whether you have a credit partner or not.

You will be asked for your login credentials for credit monitoring. Any service will work, but try to use one with FICO scores. You should also make sure you have access to all three reporting agency reports, TransUnion, Experian, and Equifax. If your monitoring service doesn't have all three, it limits how much you can get approved for.

After a review of your reports, most of the best sources will give you an initial range of how much you might get approved for reasonably quickly, within 24 hours or 48 hours from starting the process. They'll do this on a consult call with you, and review all terms and details you should know. If you want to proceed, you'll sign their agreements. Once you sign, they usually start applying within 2-3 days and start getting initial approvals quickly. Remember, some sources will get denials and have to negotiate for approvals. It can take additional days or weeks. Once they get initial approvals, it usually takes 1-2 weeks to get your cards. So typically, you'll go from applying to funding in three weeks or less.

As you get your cards, you'll get invoiced. You pay the invoice and then wait for additional cards. Good companies will give you your unique logins, so you can track their progress live as it's happening as well. So you'll know your cards are on their way.

After you get your cards, most good sources will help you call to get your limits raised. They do this by using the other cards you got approved for and create competition. So the source wants to give you higher limits than their competition to win you over.

After six months, you can then follow this same process with that source to get even more unsecured credit. Just be careful, don't put too many inquiries on your report, or it ruins your ability to get more credit.

The 0% credit card program is a significant funding solution for many entrepreneurs. You can get money as a startup or high-risk industry if you lack cash flow or collateral, and even without financials, making it easier to get approved. Also, the funding is reasonably fast, within three weeks or less. Plus, this is one of the only ways you can genuinely get 50-150k+ within a few weeks or less. So it's fast, easy money.

Just be on the lookout for some of the things to look for, and don't choose a bad company, or you'll wait longer and get less money. If you would like to apply for the best sources, you can do so here. We won't charge you for applying or when you get your funds either. You can work with our expert finance team to help you along the way, at absolutely no cost to you whatsoever.

Also, keep in mind, we do offer many other funding programs and business credit if you don't have good personal credit as this program requires. We still have options for you that can work now without needing to pay upfront for credit repair.

Chapter 6
Capital and Financing for Small and Mid-Sized Businesses

"A big business starts small."

-Richard Branson

Just as Branson said it, every business is small in the beginning. With time and constant effort that business turns into a fortune 500 company. The truth is that these small and mid-sized enterprises are the backbone of an economy. Generally, in a growing economy, there is a higher percentage of SMEs when compared to large businesses.

These businesses play a vital role in building up an economy. A small or mid-sized enterprise is such a firm that has annual revenues of under $10 million. Recently, the trend of entrepreneurship seems to have taken prevalence in society. The business environment is full of new opportunities to explore. Young and passionate entrepreneurs strive to turn their unique ideas into complete up and running businesses. Most of these businesses also start on a small or mid-sized scale. Everyone knows that one of the most basic needs of starting a business is having sufficient capital. Other than capital, a business needs frequent finances to conduct its day to day operations.

The majority of businesses out there are often hindered by the lack of finances to execute vibrant projects. These companies must eliminate such projects that will otherwise contribute positively to the bottom line of the company. I wouldn't say that finances cannot be raised for keeping a business running smoothly.

Instead, the problem is that many managers of small and medium-sized companies lack the knowledge of the variety of ways that funds can be raised to carry out additional business activities. For financing SMEs, we must elect suitable sources of funding and capitalizing. These sources can prevent companies from running into financial difficulties. I would say there is no second thought or opinion that financing is a vital tool for the growth of any firm. It is essential for entrepreneurs to access the right kind of funding, according to the needs of the firms. The firm's financial needs are of vital importance because it can shape their access to finance for small and medium enterprises. But before I explain suitable funding sources for SMEs, let me talk about small and medium-sized companies and their characteristics. Small and medium enterprises represent a large share of ventures and employment in the private sector of most economies.

SMEs form the foundation and backbone of all economies. They are also known as key segments and players in social improvement and development. These firms in markets are like productive job generators. They are the seeds for developing large organizations along with working as the oil of national, financial engines. The sector of SMEs has the upper hand on big businesses in terms of employment creation. Such companies play an active part in economic growth and development of nations, in general. They have been exceedingly underlining the importance of market advancement. SMEs are a noteworthy wellspring of financial improvement in creating societies because they assume a crucial part in the economic progress of developed countries. In reality, there are quite a few potential sources of finance for SMEs. Many of these sources have practical problems that can limit their usefulness. I have discussed some critical sources along with their limitations:

Sources

Most people go to their conventional bank when they need a business loan. However, the majority of business financing isn't coming from the big banks. Instead, I would say almost all business loans are now coming from alternative lenders. There are multiple sources of financing for SMEs. Some of these are listed as:

Retained Earnings

The first funding source that you can use is called retained earnings. People can finance their projects using funds that have been withheld from previous periods' earnings of other companies. This is referred to as the cheapest form of financing that a business can fall to first before looking outside of the company. The retained earnings can benefit you in financing your projects using funds that have been withheld from the previous period's earnings.

Leasing

The second type of funding source that you can use for your SMEs is leasing. Leasing is used for crediting and funding for small assets. I would say it could either be finance or operating lease. Remember, the benefits of using this source of the fund includes the right to engage in off-balance-sheet financing. However, the advantage of this type of funding is diminishing, as the accounting standard setters are proposing to make suitable changes that will make it almost impossible for operating lease to be practical.

Secured Loans

The third source of funding is secured loans. These loans depend on the nature of the assets because it may be possible to obtain a loan tied to that asset. This is the direct opposite of floating loans. The floating rate fund invests in bonds and debt instruments whose interest payments fluctuate with an underlying interest rate level. Companies are springing up many finance options in recent times. These will help in targeting the needs of small companies. This way, it can benefit SMEs in attracting wealth through secured funding.

Grants by Government

Before I explain this type of funding, let me introduce grants to you. Grant is a sum of money given to an individual for a specific project or purpose. In this type of funding, entrepreneurs must meet some conditions. These goals are related to cash flows and industry targets. Like, there are some cash flow implications to this particular form of raising capitals for your SMEs.

Venture Capitalists

To fund your SME, you can pick the venture capitalist option because these are the companies that set out some money periodically to invest in risky yet promising investments. The most exciting aspect of this source is that Google and some other big shots have recently joined the league. These companies offer money to startups in expectations of abnormally high returns. As a result, they enjoy monetary benefits from the sale of their interest in the company to the general public or via an initial public offer (IPO). This can also relate to another company in the trade. The organizers screen excellent investment opportunities and possibilities for entrepreneurial teams from the ones that are bad. This implies that an SME wanting to raise funds through this mean must meet specific standards. These standards will decide if you are eligible for obtaining funding or not.

Business Angels

Business angels are not actually one company or investment source. Instead, this is usually a group of wealthy individuals that specializes in investing in startups and small businesses. This is similar to the venture capitalist. The only difference is that business angels are usually individuals, while VCs typically run as firms. This way, you get the chance to fund your business and start your firm. Business angels are always specializing in funding startups, which make it easy for people like you to start your company. Remember, once a business angel is interested, they can become quite useful to the SME. They will often have an excellent business acumen themselves and likely to have many valuable and essential contacts.

Mortgages

A mortgage is another form of funding that SMEs can use for funding their businesses. Wondering how it works? Well, non-current assets like buildings can be financed through this method. This form of financing might not be suitable for all types of small businesses. Usually, there are still hurdles that need to be crossed to get money. These forms of financing can help you in funding business operations.

Alternative Investment Market

Another source of investment is called the alternative investment market (AIM)/ Second Tier market flotation. This is an essential form of capital funding where users fund their startups because they don't have access to the full-fledged capital market for their financing needs. This way, you can get investment for your startups from unconventional sources. In such scenarios, marketers don't have access to suitable funding sources for their startups.

Fulfilling their financing needs becomes the core challenge for them. The alternate methods can also employ factoring and discounting. I would say both of these sources of finance effectively let a company raise money against the security of their outstanding receivables. Again, remember that this type of financing source is only short-term, and it is often more expensive than an overdraft. I think one of the features of these sources of finance is that as an SME grows, their outstanding receivable will also expand.

Enterprise Capital Funds

To finance or fund your startup, you have the option of going to enterprise capital funds (ECF). This body was launched in the UK back in 2005. Ultimately, this is equivalent to the small business investment company of the US that has been around for around forty-seven years now. ECF has successfully supported the early growth of companies like Apple, Intel, AOL, and

FedEx in the past.

Funds from Personal Networks

An informal network of friends may include some weak ties that can come from our friends. These sources of funding can help us in forming social relationships. Surprisingly, we often neglect such sources of finance and funds for small and medium-sized companies. These investments are so powerful that up to £500,000.00 can be collected through this medium if well harnessed.

Trade Credit

SMEs can take credit from their suppliers. This is only short-term and indeed if their suppliers are larger companies who have identified them as a potentially risky and dangerous for SMEs. This way, the ability to stretch the credit period may be limited using this method.

Business Credit for SMEs

Business credit platforms connect business owners

with investors. Businesses or startup owners set up an online profile that contains all necessary details about the business and its finances. The features may include:

- An overview of the company
- Elevator pitch
- Financing history
- Business plan
- Profile of all business owners

The platforms also contain a fundraising goal, the launch date, and the end of the campaign. Investors create their profiles on these platforms to become eligible for investing. Some platforms tend to take a percentage of the funds raised as a fee. The great thing about Business credit is that both accredited and non-accredited investors can invest in it. Changes made by the Securities and Exchange Commission (SEC) in 2015 allowed the general public to invest in new businesses and startups by Business credit.

According to the SEC, businesses can only raise capital to $1.07 million through Business credit every year. Likewise, many business credit platforms have maximum and minimum limits for the amount of investment that ranges from $1 million to $15 million.

The following are some of the top Business credit platforms to consider:

Crowdfundme

It has a vast network of over 12,000 angel investors and venture capitalists. However, it is an expensive platform. Business owners have to pay $299 a month to connect with investors.

Circle Up

You have to fill an application form to become a member of CircleUp. This platform generally works with businesses that generate profit between $1 million to $15 million annually. It only accepts applications from those businesses who are looking to raise between $1 million to $10 million of capital in equity. It evaluates all applications using Helio, which decides whether the business is good enough to gain the attention of famous investors.

Fundable

Fundable only entertains accredited investors. It also works with companies that want to raise capital ranging from $50,000 to $10 million. Funder allows product-based businesses to create rewards-based campaigns for raising funds between $1,000 and $50,000.

However, Fundable does not entertain every startup. It has a pretty limited industry set. It offers its services to brewing companies, manufacturers of alcoholic beverages, timeshare companies, and travel agencies, among others.

SeedInvest

SeedInvest only accepts one percent of the startups that apply to register on this platform. It takes applications from businesses with a valuation ranging from $2 million to $4 million. If a business campaign is successful, then SeedInvest charges a placement fee of up to 7.5 percent out of the funds raised and 5 percent of the equity fee.

WeFunder

WeFunder is a platform made for people who want to invest in small-dollar denominations. Anyone from family members, friends and fans can invest, starting at only $100. It doesn't have any limits for the size of the business that wants to raise capital on this platform. Its only requirement is that the business is a for-profit company. There is no demand for an upfront fee; instead, businesses pay 7 percent of the funds they raise to cover the investment contract costs, legal work, and other expenses.

Republic

Republic is a part of a big family of startup platforms, including Product Hunt, Coinlist, and AngelList. It has an impressive 95 percent success rate for its campaigns. Any small business can start with a quick online application on Republic's website. However, there is a fee to get in, and that is around $3,000. And after reaching the funding goal, businesses must also pay a fee of 6 percent of the funds raised.

Business credit includes a collective effort of

individuals for supporting findings started by other organizations. The investor in business credit enjoys the receipt of the shares of a company in its early stages, in exchange for an agreed-upon return. This has the potential to create an innovative company with hundreds of private shareholders. These small-scale investors agree to the idea the issuer/company represents and are willing to take the risk for establishing and investing the initial seed capital the required business entity desires. Donation-based crowdfunding campaigns have no financial returns for contributors. These crowdfunding initiatives often include exceptional circumstances, such as fundraising for disaster relief, paying medical bills of the underprivileged, and other non-profit causes. These types of crowdfunding companies or platforms are available across the globe. Many investors offer money to businesses and receive ownership accordingly.

They invest because they believe in the concept and aim to profit from its expected success. This is in stark contrast to financial institutions (e.g., banks) that have stringent investment practices and who only invest in risk-controlled ventures. Business credit shows a potential for a viable startup, which is seeking relatively small investment for its business development. Purchasing shares in a startup company, in legal terms, is similar to buying shares in any other private company. The purchase of shares makes you a shareholder, which, in turn, entitles the investor to receive a percentage of company profits and enjoy partial ownership benefits.

An investor will also receive the right to make follow-on investments, and in some cases, the right to vote. Business credit allows you to invest in early-stage companies. This investment will require you to take principle risks. Losing capital is a substantial risk that all Business credit investors will risk. For example, most startups and early-stage businesses fail. Should this happen, you will lose all of your invested capital. On the other hand, business credit still has a higher potential for a return on investment if a startup venture achieves success. As a company increases its financial footprint, the chance for exponential growth could lead to gains of astronomical proportions.

Previously, potential small issuers collected funding from startup loans, grants, venture capitalists, and angel investors. These funding methods were time-consuming for entrepreneurs and required voluminous amounts of effort. The most challenging aspect of obtaining traditional funding is persuading investors to take part in innovative but potentially risky ventures. The launch of the new equity crowdfunding rules opened doors for potential entrepreneurs because they could now collect funds from many investors, who possessed a higher probability in genuinely believing in the business idea. The global acceptance of crowdfunding has transformed the investment climate in this era, as it makes finding investors relatively more fluid. It also ensures that you, as an owner, can work with other people who share the same business ideas. When equity investors work with innovators, they show their belief, which results in validating the business idea among the greater investment community. Crowdfunding shows that numerous investors have already endorsed a business model.

This validation encourages entrepreneurs to get more investment for their firms and reduces the failure rate of new business ideas. After the financial crisis in 2008, banks rejected the loan requests of more than half of small businesses and returned them empty-handed. It has been a decade since the financial crisis, and the situation remains the same. The starved small business industry has found equity-based crowdfunding as an excellent financing option, which remains a risk-free option. The shift in funding strategies in the US has encouraged SMEs to enter crowdfunding practices. These businesses often depend on a single person. Crowdfunding has enabled small ventures to launch and establish working firms. These statistics reveal how SMEs are playing a significant role in creating jobs and improving economies in the country with the help of innovative investment avenues. With traditional funding practices, SMEs would never have hit these numbers. Thus, crowdfunding investment is opening doors for the economic development of a nation. It often goes beyond the confines of country borders.

The launch of funding websites has strengthened

crowdfunding's position as a proven investment alternative available for entrepreneurs. Formerly, authorities and other concerned entities would only invest in projects that had a high ratio of success, well-defined through traditional accounting means. This made it difficult for innovators to change the business landscape by launching unique ideas. However, the launch of crowdfunding has transformed the basics of investment decisions for investors, as the viability of a business idea can now guarantee funding for professionals and novices alike. Crowdfunding has changed the suitability of investments for the entire tech industry. For example, before crowdfunding, only B2B businesses attracted crowdfunds, as it was difficult to approach people for smaller companies run by individuals.In traditional fundraising, investors look forward to receiving a specific amount as the investment return. However, crowdfunding is usually distinct, which eases the investment return policy for entrepreneurs. They can often ask for investment based on business objectives instead of depending on purely financial ones.

The new regulations of crowdfunding create a regime to govern equity crowdfunding for potential entrepreneurs. The SEC (Securities and Exchange Commission) adopts these rules under Title III of the JOBS Act of 2012. It would not be wrong to say the crowdfunding opportunities have rewritten the rules of generating funds and are now widely accepted by the regulatory authorities as well. Entrepreneurs often had to look for traditional investments before crowdfunding became a viable option.

In conventional funding, credit cards, bank loans, personal savings, family, and friends represent the most popular ways to fund a business startup. However, it is challenging to launch a business without the help of capital, which is often difficult to arrange with the traditional methods. Equity crowdfunding is now a viable option and allows many investors to empower new and old businesses alike. The new funding rules bring investors and creators closer and bridge the gap between innovation and application.

In the past, entrepreneurs had to prepare presentations, reports, and speeches to deliver their ideas and attract potential investors. The crowdfunding has made it easier to approach the investors. Now, they can make a single dedicated effort for describing their business by creating an online campaign for crowdfunding, although it is still possible to use conventional means to advertise their concept to a broader audience.

Mistakes You Make in Obtaining Business Credit

What do you need to remember while obtaining business credit? This is the question that people often ask me during my meetups and interactions with them. What I want to tell them is that you need to avoid making business credit mistakes to protect your profit margin.

Remember, using business credit to manage daily expenses can be a great way to maintain the running costs. It can help you build a margin into your cash flow and earn valuable rewards on the purchases you are already making. If you aren't putting in the thought to do your research, you need to set strict boundaries around your business.

Protecting your profit margins by making sure you avoid these top six common mistakes with your business credit card.

Picking the Wrong Type of Credit Cards

First things first, the most serious mistake that you need to avoid is choosing the wrong type of credit card. Note that not all credit cards are created equal. Business credit cards and personal credit cards are different products, even though they carry various legal protections. They have a different impact on our credit score. I would say if you are hoping to build business credit for SMEs, so that you can seek other forms of financing in the future, using a personal credit card can help you manage your business spending. It won't help you achieve that target.

On the other hand, personal credit cards carry a higher level of protection for consumers from a legal standpoint. There are some government-imposed regulations that we have on interest rates. They provide higher benefits to individual use credit.

Mixing Business and Personal Expenses

The second most crucial mistake that you need to avoid is mixing business and personal expense. Remember, it is the first piece of advice that any bookkeeper, veteran, and accountant owner will give you. I am repeating it here considering the importance of its repetition. Remember, you have to keep your business and personal spending separate from each other. If you fail to do so, you will face severe challenges when it comes to paying taxes. Also, not to forget the potential for increased scrutiny from the IRS.

Spending without a Plan

When you are getting started with a small business, particularly with a high limit business credit card in hand, it is useful for almost every potential expense to turn into an absolute need. Spending without a plan can turn challenging for you in the long run. Therefore, I would suggest you need that state of the art piece of equipment. It couldn't possibly pick up a used substitute or alternative for you. Note that you need to plan your spending according to your needs.

Not Knowing Interest Rate Changes

The most common mistake that most people make is ignoring interest rate changes. To learn about this mistake, assume that if I get an introductory offer that can be a huge benefit for business owners when you're just getting started and need a little working capital boost for those early days expenses. This opportunity will work if you're paying strict attention to the fine print, as when the introductory period ends, your interest rate will go high. If you don't know about this interest, you will end up facing issues in obtaining business credit.

Not following Payment Schedules

Of course, all those warnings you get about overspending and paying attention to your credit all comes down to this one fatal flow – getting behind on your business credit card payments. It is a terrible mistake one can make. This is an apparent incident in the abstract, but when you get down to the day to day of running your business, it happens way too easy for you. Here, I would suggest you take the time to create a budget and a cash flow forecast.

Further, you need to add payment reminders to your calendar, so you don't miss anything. I would also recommend you to go and set up an automatic payment using a suitable credit card provider. This will enable you to maintain a minimum balance in your bank account to cover it.

Wrong Approach to Business Credit Card Rewards

Many different business credit cards offer a wide array of awards and opportunities for their customers. This can save you money and make that lifestyle of an entrepreneur a little more enjoyable. Assume that if you aren't using them correctly, business credit card rewards can hurt you a lot more than they help.

Chapter 7
Maintaining an Immaculate Business Credit Score

The first rule of operating a business is to keep an extraordinary business credit score. Why is it so? Why is it that people emphasize maintaining a good business credit score? The answer to that is quite simple. If you've ever run a business, then you must be aware of the fact that to meet your day to day business tasks, you need finances. In the majority of the situations, you won't have enough cash in your business to fulfill those business requirements.

However, if you don't perform such operations just because of the insufficiency of finances, then that can use your business some severe damage. To avoid such circumstances, you will need to acquire some cash from a bank or lenders, as a loan. We all know that a business is all about seizing the opportunity and the moment. A delay in the acquisition of a loan can cost you significant losses. Therefore, if you have maintained a good credit score, the lenders will not take too long in granting you a loan. Before you can learn the ways to keep a perfect credit score, you will first need to grasp a complete understanding of what a credit score is and what kinds of credit scores are there for you. When you acquire a business credit card, you automatically start generating a credit score, whether you are aware of it or not. Your business credit score is entirely reliant on your adherence to the terms and conditions of the business credit card that you use.

The score is determined based on your credit card payment record. It is just like your FICO score, which is for your credit card. As you might know, it is a well-known credit scoring system. It makes an accurate estimation of your creditworthiness. Your mortgage, your car lease, education loans, and basically, any other kind of loan you wish to acquire is granted after keen consideration of your creditworthiness. Similarly, a business credit score also determines the creditworthiness of your business.

It receives a credit score after the credit report of your company has been carefully reviewed. If you get a higher business credit score, it refers to the fact that your business has been consistent in making timely payments to the creditors. Throughout the book, I have been emphasizing on the fact that building a strong business credit line requires you to make sure that you pay your creditors on time. This is the first rule for securing a higher credit score. Before we get into the details about business credit score, I would first like you to be clear on what a personal FICO score is.

FICO is a business analytics software company and is based in San Jose, California. Bill Fair and Earl Issac founded the firm in 1956. Their FICO score has become the leading credit score used to determine consumer credit risk. William Fair, one of the founders, was an engineer by trade. Earl Isaac was another founder and was a mathematician by profession. The two met while working at the Stanford Research Institute in Menlo Park, California. In 1958, FICO pitched their first credit risk analysis system to 50 American lenders.

The organization went public in 1986 and currently trades traded on the New Your Stock Exchange under the ticker symbol FICO. The company debuted its first general-purpose FICO score in 1989. Ratings are based on credit reports and range from 300 to 850. Lenders use the scores to gauge a potential borrower's creditworthiness. Fannie Mae and Freddie Mac first began using FICO scores to help determine which American consumers qualified for mortgages bought and sold by the companies in 1995.

Called Fair, Isaac, and Company, this name was changed to Fair Isaac Corporation in 2003. The company rebranded again in 2009 and is now called FICO, making their name the same, as the signature FICO score they offer.

FICO Services include the following:

- Customer acquisition analytics

- Debt management and collection analytics

- Fraud and security analytics

- Risk analysis scoring

- Customer decision making and analytic data solutions

The FICO score uses a mathematical model that is used to depict a consumer's risk of going 90 days late on an account within the next 24 months. Lenders use this measure to help them make billions of credit decisions every year. FICO calculates these scores based solely on the information in consumer credit reports maintained at the credit reporting agencies.

This crucial credit score is calculated by a mathematical equation that evaluates the information present in your credit report at various credit reporting agencies. By comparing this information to the patterns in hundreds of thousands of past credit reports, the FICO score estimates your level of future credit risk.

You have three FICO credit scores, one for each of the three credit bureaus: Equifax, TransUnion, and Experian. Each FICO Score is based on information the credit bureau keeps on file about you. The FICO Score from each credit reporting agency considers only the data in your credit reports at that agency. Your credit score may be different at each of the leading credit reporting agencies. If your current scores from the credit reporting agencies are different, it's because the information those agencies have on you differs. If your data is identical at all three credit reporting agencies, each FICO Score should be similar.

For your FICO Score to be calculated, your credit report with the bureau from which you want your score must contain enough information—and enough recent information—on which to base your credit score. Generally, that means you must have at least one account that has been working for six months or longer, and at least one account that has been reported to the credit reporting agency within the last six months.

There are MANY credit scores out there. There are credit scores consumers can pull themselves through credit monitoring, mortgage scores, auto scores, and many more activities. There are actually over 16 different credit *"scorecards"* that exist today with FICO alone. Each of these scorecards will reflect different credit scores. These scorecards are designed to help particular industries better gauge credit risk.

The mortgage industry, for example, is more concerned with a consumers' past mortgage history than anything else, so they weight home loan history heavier into the total score calculation than other accounts, and thus a consumer's credit monitoring score might be 660. But then when they apply for a mortgage, their score might be much lower due to some past negative mortgage accounts on the report. Their mortgage score might even be higher than their consumer score if they have positive mortgage accounts.

A credit score that a consumer pulls themselves will not be the same as their Mortgage Industry Option Score, the scores lenders and brokers use to access mortgage default risk. Their mortgage score won't be the same as their auto score that car dealers pull either which is known as the Auto Industry Option Score, because the auto score weighs past auto history heavier into the score makeup versus consumer scores. These different credit scorecards are designed to help specific industries better determine risk. As many sectors offer credit, there are also just as many credit scores available for them to find the risk associated with a personal or business credit consumer. Plus, different scores are offered by various companies creating even more credit scores. FICO is the biggest provider of consumer credit scores. But now even the credit bureaus themselves are in the credit scoring game, providing their Vantage Score. The three top credit bureaus released their scoring system on 14th March 2006. All three leading credit reporting agencies use the same formula to calculate the Vantage Score which has scores as high as 990 while FICO scores can only be as high as 850. So even though a 700 FICO score reflects good consumer credit, whereas a 700 Vantage score reflects below-average personal credit.

Scores going up to 990 versus FICO scores going up to 850 have created an issue with lenders. This is one of the main reasons that Vantage Score hasn't become widely accepted, so the bureaus have now changed their score range with Vantage Score 3.0, which was released in 2013. With the new Vantage Score, scores only go as high as 850, mimicking the FICO top score. Fair Isaac and Vantage Score hold their credit scoring formulas as a close secret, much like the formula for Coca-Cola or your grandma's legendary double chocolate-chip cookies. This can be quite frustrating for consumers when they see remarks on the credit report like *"too many revolving debt accounts"* and not knowing precisely what that means. Fortunately, Fair Isaac and Vantage Score have issued some public information about how they calculate credit scores.

Factors on Which Fair Isaac and Vantage Score Determine Credit Score
Payment History

Lenders wish to learn more about a person's payment history, which is why both Fair Isaac and Vantage Score consider it. Payment history is broken down into the following subcategories:

- **Recency** refers to the last time a payment was late. The more time that passes, the better are the scores.
- **Frequency** is the number of late payments of a person. One late payment looks a heck of a lot better than a dozen.

- **Severity** is the number of days for which a person has defaulted on his debt. A payment 30 days late is not as severe as a payment, 60 or 120-days late.
- Collections, tax liens, foreclosures, repossessions, charge-offs, and bankruptcies are credit score killers.

As I mentioned before, you can improve this aspect of your score by paying your bills on time. Also, the more accounts you have paid as agreed to offset the ones you don't will help your score. So, if you do have late payments reporting on your credit, you can offset these by adding new positive accounts and making sure you have a lot of considerations you are paying as agreed… to counteract the accounts not paid as agreed.

How Much Is Owed

The score looks at the total amount owed on all accounts as well as how much you owe on different types of accounts (mortgage, auto, and others). Using a higher percentage of the credit limits will worry lenders and hurt the credit score. People who max out their limits have a much higher risk of default.

Utilization

When it comes to revolving debt credit cards, the formula looks at the difference between the high limit and balances. For Example, let's say your customer has a MasterCard with a credit limit of $10,000, and they have spent $2,000 of it. This is a 20% utilization ratio, and the lower the ratio, the higher the credit score. So, if you are looking for a quick credit score boost, pay down any accounts you can.

With FICO, 30% of your credit score is based on utilization, while 35% is based on payment history. Utilization is the second-highest weighted aspect of your scores. This means if you are over-utilizing your revolving accounts, you can damage your scores as much as if you were paying your payments late each month. Anything over 30% of your limit being used will lower your credit scores. Adding credit cards to your report with higher limits can also SIGNIFICANTLY and quickly raise your scores, sometimes as much as 100 points or more.

One more important tidbit, CLOSED ACCOUNTS do not help and can hurt if there is a balance remaining. A long, perpetuated myth has been to close accounts that are not in use, but this will hurt consumers in several ways. As you now know, overall and individual account utilization plays a significant role in credit scoring - if consumers close old accounts, your overall utilization rate will increase, which will cause their score to decrease.

Length of Credit History/ Depth of Credit

This is less significant than the previous factors, but it still matters. It considers (1) the age of the oldest account and (2) the average age of all your accounts. It is possible to have a good score with a short history, but typically the longer the history, the better.

Young people, students, and others can still have high credit scores as long as the other factors are positive with FICO. This is the third most vital aspect of score calculation. If a person is new to credit, then there is little they can do to improve a credit score. No newly added accounts can be back-dated to improve this score aspect, and you can get added as an authorized user to a family member's account that has been in long-standing, and that can improve this aspect of your score. The average age of accounts is another essential reason to keep all accounts open. If a consumer has multiple accounts they've had for some time, but don't use - they are still benefiting from the average age of the accounts open in their credit file. Also, make sure you use each of your accounts, at least once every six months.

Credit issuers must reserve the money offered in credit limits for their clients' use, so they don't like having accounts sitting dormant that are not making them money. If an account lies dormant for a long enough time, many creditors will cancel the account due to inactivity. Additionally, a credit reporting agency will calculate an account as inactive if there has not been any activity in the most recent six month period of time. A dormant account does not benefit your score as much as an active account.

New Credit / Recent Credit

New credit is not always a bad thing. However, opening new accounts can hurt a credit score, particularly if a consumer applies for lots of credit in a short time and doesn't have a long credit history. A personal credit score may also be dependent on the number of accounts a consumer has recently applied for.

The number of accounts a consumer has newly opened, and the time that has passed since the consumer applied for a loan are both vital. The time that has passed since the consumer opened the account also affects the credit score a lot.

Difference between Personal FICO Score and Business Credit Score

Do not confuse yourself, thinking that a personal FICO score is the same as your business credit score.

Score Range

Although they might seem similar, the significant difference between them is that they both have different scoring ranges. A personal FICO score ranges between 300 to 850, whereas a business credit score may lie within the scope of 0 to 100. Generally, a business credit score of 80 or above is considered to be very good, which will make it easier for you to acquire loans from various lenders. This is vital for most small businesses.

Access to Credit Score

A business credit score is determined by three major business credit bureaus. Equifax, Dun & Bradstreet, and Experian review a business's credit report and then grant a credit score as per their specific conditions. However, these bureaus charge you a significant amount to discuss your business's or company's credit report and tell you, your business credit score according to it.

On the other hand, a consumer can know his or her credit score once a year for free. Consumer credit bureaus like TransUnion, Experian, and Equifax do not even charge consumers for reviewing their credit reports and determine the personal FICO score, utterly free of cost.

Standardization

To calculate a consumer credit score, the majority of consumer credit bureaus apply the algorithms of the FICO system. In the case of business credit score, every business credit bureau uses different algorithms, whichever may seem fit to them, by considering the credit report of the business or the company.

Privacy

The privileges of privacy lack in a business credit score as all the information about a company's business credit score are public. Whereas, your personal FICO score can only be seen by you and a few selected parties.

Data

Your accounts and credit cards have no part in your

business credit reports. A business credit score is usually determined on the review of all the statements of accounts that exist under the company's name. Similarly, the personal credit score is calculated on the analysis of your personal accounts and credit card activity. They both remain separate from each other under most scenarios.

The difference between a personal FICO score and a business credit score will become more transparent to you after I have enlightened you on how a business credit score is determined.

Calculation of Business Credit Score

So let's get down to the specifics. As I mentioned before, there are three major business credit bureaus which determine a company's credit score, Equifax, Experian, and Dun & Bradstreet. All of these bureaus have their unique methods and ways of calculating a business's creditworthiness.

There are several other business credit reporting agencies as well, but the ones mentioned here are the most popular and most reliable. Whenever you approach one of these bureaus to have your business credit reports reviewed, make sure you keep the following factors under consideration.

- **The collection and verification of information are done by each bureau in its own specific manner.** Generally, business credit card issuers, vendors, banks, and data-gathering trade associations are approached by bureaus for the data on payment history. Then third parties are also contacted to verify the information that has been collected.

- **Make sure you double-check your company's business credit report.** Even though business credit bureaus give complete assurance that they have carefully collected all the information, but you still might be able to spot a few mistakes in the report. Whenever you spot such issues with your business credit report, be sure to contact the bureau with evidence that the information they collected was incorrect. Once you provide them with proper reasoning, the bureau will go ahead and rectify your business credit report.

Experian Business Credit Score

Keeping these two factors in mind, let's imagine that you first went to Experian to get your business credit reports reviewed and see how much your company can score. Experian uses a very unique business credit score model while evaluating your business credit reports.

This model is known as the Intelliscore Plus, which provides a result in a simple 1 to 100 score range. The efficiency and precision of this model can be judged by the fact that it takes under account, about 800 variables while evaluating a business score. It gives the lenders and banks a bird's eye vision of not only a business's payment trends but also the business owner's consumer data.

Although, while the evaluation of a business credit score, the owner's personal credit history is not made a part of assigning a business credit score to the company, but it does leave an impact on the lenders about how the business owner maintains his own credit score. Experian considers Intelliscore Plus to be a reliable way of calculating a company's business credit score due to the following factors.

- It provides a complete overview of the company. The financial history of the company, collections, payment trends, and public record filings; all of these factors are mentioned in the score and report presented by Intelliscore Plus.

- All of the data upon which the business credit score is dependent and collected by the company through third parties. Intelliscore Plus does not take self-reported data while calculating the score.

- Specifically, considering the cases of small businesses, a blended score is much required to evaluate a company's financial standing accurately. Therefore, Intelliscore Plus produces a score, which takes into account not only data on the business but also on the business owner.

Still not clear on how Experian is determining your business credit score? Well, of course, you aren't. I haven't told you the real thing yet. The first thing you need to remember is that your company's history of previous loans and debts is most crucial to any Business

Credit Bureau you'll ever go to. This is the first thing they will check while reviewing your business credit reports. So Experian also checks if you have completely paid off your previous debts, or if you still have some amount outstanding.

Moving on, the second factor Experian will consider will be the amount of debt you still owe to other creditors. It is probable that your creditors will be approached by Experian to see how your company's relation with them has been. Remember, a happy creditor means higher business credit score. So you need to maintain good relationships with your creditors.

The number of times your company has taken loans or borrowed money from lenders can also be a significant factor. Also, the size of your company, whether it's a small business enterprise or a mid-sized business, can affect your company's business credit score. The time it has been since your company has been established is also considered to be a contributing factor in the calculation of your business credit score.

Apart from all these factors, bear in mind that credit reporting agencies approach every entity, which might have any information regarding your business. Similarly, Experian may also contact state filing offices, collection companies, marketing databases, and legal filings to collect data regarding your business finances and credit use.

Equifax Business Credit Score

Equifax opts for a scoring technique which is a little different from that of Experian. The business credit score presented by Equifax is based on three different scores. As mentioned earlier, your payment history is essential in the evaluation of your business credit score. So the first score of Equifax's scoring system is **A Payment Index Score.** Your company's payment history for the previous year is evaluated by Equifax.

Based on the data and information, it can collect from small business lenders, public records, and trade records. You should try to make your payments to the lenders on time. Otherwise, it becomes a detractor for your business credit score. Equifax pays attention to how vigilant your company is in making timely payments to the lender. Late payments lower your business credit score.

The score range for a payment index score is between 1 and 100. The second score in this scoring technique is **a credit risk score**. Equifax determines your business's ability to repay its debts by carefully reviewing its history. The size of your company, credit limits, and the credit history of your company with lenders and banks suggest the probability of your business paying off its debts. This scoring range is from 100 to 992. The higher the score, the more its likelihood of paying back the creditors. Last but not least, Equifax also takes into account the likelihood of your company, making it through the year. Considering your company's history of late payments and for how long the oldest financial accounts of your business have existed, Equifax scores the probability of your business's failure.

This score will go from 1,000 to 1,880, depending on the information gathered from supplier invoices and your company's current use of credit. This is called **a business failure score**. These three scores awarded to your company by Equifax are reviewed by the lenders and based on that, they grant or deny your request for a loan.

Dun & Bradstreet Credit Score

Dun & Bradstreet, often called D&B, is the most significant business credit reporting agency, about ten times larger than Experian or Equifax. They provide information on businesses and corporations for use in credit decisions worldwide. It is a publicly-traded company (DNB) on NYSE, with headquarters in Short Hills, New Jersey. D&B has roots that track back to 1841, with the formation of the Mercantile Agency in New York. This was 50 years before the first consumer agency Equifax was born. In 1933, the Mercantile Agency joined with R.G. Dun & Company and became known as Dun and Bradstreet of today. Four US Presidents were former employees of Mercantile Agency, which later became D&B. They are Abraham Lincoln, Ulysses S. Grant, Grover Cleveland, and William McKinley. All of them worked as credit reporters.

There are a couple of steps you'll need to take to set up your business first before you contact D&B about your business credit. The <u>first step</u> is to set up your business entity. You can build credit with any entity. But you'll want to consider either a **corporation** or **LLC** to help reduce personal liability in the business. With Sole Proprietors and Partnerships, you ARE the business; you're the same. In those cases, <u>you'll always be liable</u> for what happens in your industry. With Corporations and LLCs, you and the firms are separate from each other, making it easier also to separate your liability. You can **set up your entity** by visiting your <u>Secretary of State website</u>. Search for the name you want to ensure it's not already taken, then follow the steps to set up a new for-profit or non-profit business. Fees vary by state, but the setup process usually only takes 15 minutes or less to complete.

Next, visit the IRS website to get your Employer ID Number or EIN. Do NOT pay for your EIN... it's **free**. Some companies who try to look official and help you get your EIN, but at the end of the process, they charge you a fee. You don't need to pay.

Business credit reporting agencies like D&B **get data** from many different places. These may include utility companies, landlords, and companies that help set up new businesses, insurance, and benefits providers, and many others. If the reporting agencies know you exist, you can have a **low credit score** even if you have no credit.

Check with D&B to see if they have a record set up for you now. It's **FREE** and easy to do this! You can go directly to D&B's website to check **iUpdate** for your business. You can always check whether you are currently set up with all three credit agencies... **all for FREE.** If you pull up a record for your business with the reporting agencies, before you take another step, you should consider pulling your actual reports. To do this, you'll need to enroll for credit monitoring. In doing so, you'll see if you have any credit reporting already on your business. You'll also know **if you have any previous scores**. And if you have negative items on your report, you can dispute those through iUpdate or monitoring.

If your search with D&B doesn't show you have

your D-U-N-S number, you'll want to **get it set up.** In 1963, the introduction of the Data Universal Numbering System or D-U-N-S helped bring business information into the computer age. Today D&B maintains a database of over 213 million companies globally. The **D-U-N-S Number** is a nine-digit number issued by Dun & Bradstreet and assigned to each business location in the D&B database, each having a unique, separate, and distinct operation for the purpose. Every business <u>must first have a D-U-N-S number</u> before Dun & Bradstreet assigns a Paydex business credit score to them. The DUNS number is the preferred method worldwide for identifying businesses. Unlike national Employment Identification Number (EIN), a D-U-N-S number may be issued to any company worldwide, making it different from traditional American identity. It is used by many <u>foreign governments,</u> including the US and Australia, the European Commission, and even the **United Nations**. More than **50** global, industry, and trade associations recognize, recommend, or require DUNS for compliance.

A Paydex Score which ranges between 1 and 100 is

used by Dun & Bradstreet to evaluate a company's credit risk. There are several data-gathering companies which are usually contacted by the bureau in the collection of data. Dun & Bradstreet collects your business's payment information from such companies to calculate your company's *"commercial credit score"* and a *"financial stress score."* Based on this score, your lenders decide the amount of credit they will grant you. This score is used by several entities like your landlords or even insurance companies to set your premiums.

Your company will be assigned a D-U-N-S number, which is a nine-digit number. It is considered as a unique identity for your company in the Dun & Bradstreet's Data Cloud. Dun & Bradstreet focuses on a more continuous and comprehensive view of your business, carefully considering your records of vendors for the past four years at least. In other words, the Paydex score needs to be high enough if you wish to attract investors and lenders. Dun & Bradstreet also suggests that businesses should make sure of timely payments and maintain a positive history with the suppliers and vendors. It stresses this by using these factors as the primary credit score calculators.

As mentioned earlier, a report presented by Dun & Bradstreet is comprised of two types of scores. Firstly, a score which ranges between 101 and 670, which is **a commercial credit score** that shows the probability of a company defaulting on payments or having the tendency of defrauding the creditors. If Dun & Bradstreet gives a lower retail credit score to a company, it means there is a higher chance of that company's delinquency. This will eventually result in that company being denied on its loan applications. Secondly, it consists of a financial stress score, which predicts whether or not your business will be able to strive in the coming year. A company generally fails to flourish when it is not able to fully pay off its debt to the creditors and closes all its business operations. This score ranges from 1,001 to 1,610. If this score turns out to be on the higher side, it may be quite improbable for such a company to survive. Higher financial stress score means that the company is more likely to dissolve in the next 12 months.

The Paydex Score ranges from **0-100**, with 100 being the best score a business can obtain. A score of **80** or higher is considered *"good"* or healthy credit. A business can earn a good business Paydex credit score by ensuring payments are made promptly to suppliers and vendors. So now that you understand how your business credit score is evaluated, you should learn a few tips on how to maintain a perfect business credit score.

How to Maintain a Perfect Business Credit Score

To maintain a good business credit score, pay close attention to the things I am about to tell you now.

Decoding Business Credit

Business credit refers to the available loan that's linked to the business's EIN. This is credit for your business, which is not linked to you personally in any possible way.

Using your business credit, you can get vendor credit cards, high-limit accounts with most major retailers, fleet credit, as well as cash credit for your business, including Visa and MasterCard.

You can get approved for business credit accounts, regardless of personal credit quality. When you build your business credit the right way, you won't even supply your SSN on the application.

With no SSN supplied, there isn't even a personal credit pull. For this reason, you can obtain high-limit business credit accounts, regardless of your personal credit... no matter how bad it may be.

Business credit is reported by the business credit reporting agencies, not the consumer reporting agencies that we are all too familiar with. As business credit is used, it has no adverse impact on the owner's consumer credit because it's not reported to consumer agencies. This means utilizing the account, even over 30% won't have any adverse impact on your personal credit scores, and there are no inquiries on the personal credit when you apply for business credit as long as you don't supply your SSN.

So you don't need to worry about your personal credit affecting your business credit score, but be vigilant about your creditors for business, as that's what matters in calculating your business credit score.

Why Using Personal Credit to Funding Your Business is a Bad Idea

You can get credit for your EIN that's not linked to your SSN. In doing so, you save yourself a lot of potential damage to your consumer credit scores. This is because 10% of your total consumer credit score is based on inquiries, so if you are using your personal credit to apply for business loans and credit, your scores will go down as a result of those inquiries. Plus, those inquiries can remain on your credit for an extended period of time, affecting your ability to borrow more money. Some unsecured business lending sources won't even lend you money if you have two inquiries or more on your personal credit reports within the last six months. 30% of your total consumer credit score is based on utilization, so if you use your personal credit to get credit cards for your business, you will lower your scores considerably.

Using more than 30% of your limit WILL result in a score decrease so if your limit is $1,000, having a balance above $300 lowers your scores. All of this means that 40% of your total score is damaged just by applying and using the credit you obtain with your consumer scores. When you use the available business credit, your score is entirely unaffected.

Know the difference between personal and business credit scores

To get good scores with business credit reporting agencies, all you need to do is get some credit that reports to these agencies. Get the credit, use the credit, and then pay the bills timely, preferably as early as possible, after you make the purchase. Early payments alone mean you'll get a high credit score. With that spectacular score, you will be able to get high-limit accounts quickly.

Consumer credit scores are made up of five factors. So it takes years of well-disciplined borrowing to get excellent scores. But business credit scores can be built much faster, because all that's needed is to have accounts reported with good payment histories.

ANYONE Can See Your Business Credit Reports

With consumer credit, someone has to have your permission to pull your credit reports. This is required under the Fair Credit Reporting Act, which requires that someone have your Permissible Purpose to pull your credit. If someone pulls your credit without your permission, they may have to pay a fine of $1,000 or more.

With consumer credit, only specific organizations get the ability even to access your credit reports such as banks, auto dealers, mortgage brokers, and others licensed to lend money. But with business credit, this information is made public, which means ANYONE who wants your business credit reports can quickly and cheaply get it. Think about some of the people who can see your reports as they wish and whenever they want. It can include customers, prospects, suppliers, and others who you might do business with competitors, and ANYONE else who wants it. Here is some of the information they can easily see about your business: the number of trade lines, credit score, high credit limits, past payment performance, employees, revenue, and much more is available to anyone.

All that's needed to pull an established credit report is the business name. If a company isn't well-established, a business address is required. So, with only a business name and address, and without needing permission, anyone can pull your business credit reports. Keep monitoring your reports regularly to see what others can know about you. Moreover, keep building your business credit, so you can have a credible image portrayed for anyone who wants to see your credit in the future, especially those who lend money or issue business credit.

No Personal Guarantee

When you put your SSN on a business credit application, you are almost always providing a personal guarantee. This means you are personally liable for your business debts. So if you were to default on one of these obligations, the creditor would pursue your business assets first, then they'll come after your personal assets, including your home, your cars, your stocks and bonds, your bank accounts, and all other assets in your name.

Business owners don't expect to fail, but unfortunately, 90% of them do. It makes no sense to put you and your family's financial future in jeopardy when you know going in that you have a 90% possibility of ruining it. Remember, many times, the reasons a business might fail have nothing to do with you, or things you can control, such as shifts in the economy and a change in the current industry trends. There is no doubt, starting and running a business is risky. This is why most conventional banks make it so hard to get a loan. So DO NOT use a personal guarantee unless you have to. With many business loans, you will need to do it, but with credit, you DON'T need it as long as you build business credit.

Business Credit Increases the Value of Your Business

Which of these two businesses would you buy that have been in existence for five years and are the same in every way? Company A has no business credit profile and score and is being recommended for no credit. Company B has ten trade lines reporting, an excellent business credit profile, and score, $52,000 in available credit to help with growth, and is being recommended for $42,000 in credit from the business reporting agencies.

Anyone who has sold or bought a business will tell you of the importance of business credit. Would you want to buy this company from what you see on the business report? Is the company *"established,"* do they pay their bills, do they look like a successful company? ANY potential investor or buyer of your business will review your business credit quality. Having excellent business credit gets you a higher evaluation, as well as makes your company more appealing to invest in or sell.

How to Get High Limit Business Credit Accounts

When you have access to more store and cash credit cards, you also have access to a lot more useable money. As per SBA, business credit limits are 10-100 times that of consumer limits. So not only can you get business credit fast, but you can also get credit with very high limits that allow you to expand your business.

This is because businesses have a greater need for credit than a consumer does. This is referred to as credit capacity. You may never need to get $10,000 in credit with Dell for home computers, but you can easily need this much or even more for a business. Obtaining business credit radically increases your available buying power. An average Staples card limit on the consumer side might be $3,000, but in the business world, it might be closer to $30,000.

It's actually quite common to get credit cards with limits of 10k or more within 2-3 months from starting to apply for credit. This is impossible to accomplish with consumer credit. Here are some actual approvals from customers' months into business credit building with a few top firms:

Apple	$12,500
Shell	$15,000
Exxon	$5,000
Office Depot	$15,000
Costco	$20,000

Sunoco	$15,000
Sears	$15,000
BP	$8,000
Amazon	$3,500

Business credit is perfect for businesses that don't have or want to show financials. Let's face it; we write off all the expenses in a company that we can. This leaves a smaller net profit, which is what most lenders and investors look at. Business credit doesn't look at financials or bank statements.

A business even with no cash flow can be approved for high limit cards, helping them grow their cash flow and achieve sustenance. Now that you have the complete knowledge of what a business credit score is, how it is calculated, and how you can maintain a perfect business credit score, the ball is in your court. This is the time you start working on your business credit score and enable your company to reach greater heights. Don't forget; higher business credit score means greater financial stability, as well as access to funds that can ensure long-term business success.

Bibliography

10 Stats That Explain Why Business Credit is Important for Small Business. (n.d.). Retrieved October 9, 2019, from https://www.sba.gov/blog/10-stats-explain-why-business-credit-important-small-business

Exploring Alternative Sources of a Business Capital Finance. (n.d.). Retrieved October 9, 2019, from https://swypefast.com/exploring-alternative-sources-business-capital-finance/

The 4 Most Common Reasons a Small Business Fails. (n.d.). Retrieved October 9, 2019, from https://www.investopedia.com/articles/personal-finance/120815/4-most-common-reasons-small-business-fails.asp